To Irving and Rose

Acknowledgments

This work has been in progress over the last six years. It started as an exercise in a writing class where I live in Ojai, California. My teacher, Deb Norton, had us write a mystery using a photograph for inspiration. This book is the story that unfolded. Thank you Deb for your creative expertise during this project.

I am indebted to my editor, Christina Wilson, for your guidance and skill.

A heartfelt thank you to Holly Carlson, Bill Fox, Robert Wolfe, Brook Masters, Andrea Owad, Laurel Davar, and Meredith Lynne Dean for your feedback and support, and to Michael Lommel for the professionalism you brought to this work when I was fumbling.

A special thank you to my dear friend, editor, and publisher, Margaret Dodd. Without you this story would never have seen the light of day.

To my husband Terry, for all the years of love, encouragement, and being my rock.

Lastly, to all those silent voices that have perished at the hands of hatred, I am grateful for your lives. I have to wonder if I heard your agonized whispers in the middle of the night. Wake me up you did, to what it is to suffer at the hands of prejudice over the color of your skin, the legacy of your genetic heritage, your sexual preference, and in many, your authentic selves that dared to differ from the norm.

"For one moment our lives met, our souls touched."
OSCAR WILDE

"One can survive everything nowadays, except death, and live down everything except a good reputation." OSCAR WILDE

Prologue

1895

Telegraphs clacked around the world with the breaking news of the conviction of Oscar Wilde. Mr. Wilde, noted celebrity and one of the most successful playwrights, novelists, poets, and short story writers, suffered a stunning defeat when he was sentenced to two years of hard labor in prison after being convicted for "gross indecency." Wilde's case, one of the first tried under Britain's recently passed Criminal Law Amendment Act, criminalized sexual activity between members of the same sex, thus changing people's attitudes about homosexuality from a mood of pity and tolerance to hatred and abuse.

The unofficial buzz in the tabloids was that Wilde was caught in the act with another male, Lord Douglas, the son of the Marquis of Queensberry, and Victorian London would have none of it. The news of trial and conviction spread fast and furiously to towns large and small around the world, exactly the kind of news story Red River Pass, a small town in Nevada, relished.

"Anyone who lives within their means suffers from a lack of imagination." OSCAR WILDE

1

In the middle of the night, in the sleepy town of Red River Pass, a lonely telegraph machine clicked away, with no one yet present to receive its message, delivering in Morse code the news of a writer in England who had just made legal history for being the first famous person convicted of *committing acts of gross indecency*. The news, significant as it was, would repeat hourly around the clock, with deciphered words setting in motion titillating gossip about homosexuality.

Red River Pass, a small Nevada town, had a similar incident of smaller magnitude several years back when a couple of local boys told lies about seeing two men hugging. This caused an upheaval in the lives of those men and their families. Some still believe the lies told were true, especially after one of the men committed suicide over the incident. Back then, two men hugging was bad enough; but now a man had been put on trial and thrown in prison for sexual activity with another man. The fact that this was now recognized in England as an illegal criminal act was sure to cause a frenzy.

※

The early morning dry cool air had just enough breeze to send a tumbleweed or two through its empty streets, as wooden sidewalks gained new cracks, and bodies stirred to wake.

Mildred Dunlap's day started, like every other, at five-thirty sunrise. While dressing she looked out her bedroom window to a place several feet from the house to notice a six-foot sagebrush move. At first she did not see anything in the sand nearby. Then at closer view she caught sight of a sage grouse browsing leaves. The plant had not yet blossomed into the tiny yellowish white flowers that would come with summer, still a few months away. She loved this time of year when spring starts, paving the way to summer, and her body surrendered to the warmth. A time when life begins to slow and relax in the heat, like a quiet that comes with the nighttime in a bustling city.

The good mood she was in abruptly ended when she went to her kitchen and found the beginning of a rat's nest at the bottom of a pantry. Twigs, leaves, bristles of pinecone, tiny particles of what looked like wood from a mesquite shrub, and a corner of a piece of fabric from a towel were alongside several droppings.

"Darn it!" she yelled, waking her cousin Edra from her sleep.

When Edra found her, she was in the kitchen on her knees. "What's …" She looked at the mess. "Oh no, I thought Ben took care of that."

"Not what I like waking up to," Mildred replied.

"I know. I know."

"Now I'll end up spending the day here cleaning this mess and try-ing to find how they're getting in." She peered in further to survey the extent of the damage and mumbled something unintelligible, then backed out in disgust. "Do I have to do everything myself?"

Edra moved closer to put a hand on Mildred's shoulder to assuage the frustration. "I can clean this up. Ben can patch the openings…you need to get the horse medicine in town."

"Ben's not coming out to work till this afternoon. If the right thing had been delivered in the first place…"

"Mil. It's just a rash on Lil," Edra commented about Mildred's horse. She knew Mildred was annoyed at having to return to town to rectify the mistake, and now this on top of it. "You hate those rats. You go to town and I'll handle this. The rest can wait till Ben gets here." Edra smiled.

Mildred softened. She didn't want to have Edra do what she herself found repulsive. "You sure?" She laughed, releasing some irritation. "I was in such a good mood when I woke up."

"By the time you get home you'll feel better."

"Yeah, you're probably right."

*

Mildred, still in a bad mood when she saw the crowd outside the telegraph office, became even more annoyed that people were milling around, not getting on with their business. When she got within earshot she heard the excited voices.

"That's disgusting! Can you imagine…they wrote love letters to each other. That turns my stomach…two men together." Sarah Funkle was not discrete in pointing her comment in the direction beyond her circle of friends, which happened to be in earshot of Mildred who was approaching.

"Two men together?" Josie Purdue raised her voice above the crowd, drawing a hush and attention to her. "More like five! All his past lovers came forth. Shows what an ungodly lot they all are. He deserves what he got. Throw away the key, that's what I say. Those kinds don't deserve to walk the face of the earth."

"Why didn't they throw them all in prison?"

"The news says 'they repented' for their crimes."

"Repent? Their words don't undo their sinful actions!" Josie was irate. "Lock 'em all away!"

The women broke their conversation when they noticed Mildred near them.

Josie gave Mildred a disapproving once-over as if to say, *With all your money, can't you do better for yourself?*

"Why, hey Mildred," greeted Sarah.

Mildred nodded and tried to continue past them.

"Did you hear the latest?" Josie directed her question at Mildred, in an uncharacteristically friendly manner.

"Ladies," Mildred did not take the bait but turned back for a moment to face them, "If you'll pardon me, I have a sick horse to tend to." She exaggerated her horse's condition as an excuse to get away. She had already heard enough.

"I tell you, that's the most disgusting thing I ever heard." Josie turned back to Sarah. "Just like with Harold Simmons and Bert Langley. And to think it happened right here in our God-fearing town. The nerve... I shudder to think what would have become of things if the Parker boys hadn't found them. That whole lot deserved what they got!"

The edge in Josie's voice with the mention of the Parker boys sent a chill down Mildred's spine. A hot flush surged through her as she recalled the incident that happened several years back. The Parker boys were out playing by the lake when they ran across Harold Simmons hugging Bert Langley. When the Parker boys ran home and told their parents, they exaggerated what they saw. "They were kissing, starting to undress..." said the younger Parker boy to his father. Within twenty-four hours two families were thrown into irreversible turmoil. "Two men don't do things like that," spread like wildfire. Five days after the incident, Harold Simmons took a gun to his head and blew his brains out. A week later, both families moved from Red River Pass.

Although she could not make full sense out of what all the commotion was about, the voices, screeching about Wilde and the Parker boys, echoed in Mildred's head as she moved through the crowd into the office where she saw Satchel Purdue busy chattering with several people from town. None of them appeared to be doing any business with him, which further irritated her. She found a spot to write the telegram she had come in to send.

"Yes, it's a busy day here. This'll keep Josie going for months," Satchel laughed, referring to his wife. "She's been at it all morning and..." The sound of ticking from the telegraph machine distracted him. "Excuse me. I better see what this is and get anything new over to Gus's public noticeboard."

Mildred knew Satchel was right about Josie. She thought of them, Josie and Satchel, going at it together. An odd couple they were: he with his tall stiff appearance befitting a telegraph operator whose glasses fogged up with the mention of his wife's name — a thin body and neck

12

that mildly bulged over a tight shirt collar supporting a face that housed wrinkles belying his age, just into his forties; and she loose in her five-foot-four figure with excessively endowed breasts and hips that drew even more attention to her shrill voice.

In contrast to Mildred, Josie thrived on being the center of attention. Outside of them both being women, there was absolutely no similarity in appearance between the two. Whereas Mildred was a large woman with a face masculine in appearance, Josie was pretty in a feminine way with curved lips and eyebrows that accentuated her blue-green eyes and overly dilated pupils seeming always to be alert like an animal stalking prey. Were Josie to have a different personality or attitude she could be beautiful, like Edra, but her demeanor was so distasteful with constant faultfinding in others that it cast a dark ugliness over her. The mere comparison of Edra to Josie, for Mildred, was like comparing good with evil, beauty with ugliness, complete opposites that had nothing desirable in common. Mildred was distracted from her thoughts by the chattering machine that was taking forever to deliver its message. The longer the ticking occurred with everyone's attention riveted on Satchel, and the more time that passed, the more aggravated she became.

"Anything?" Several in the room kept asking while Mildred contained her fury and waited for him to finish.

Satchel took notes on the dots and dashes then turned to the group with a disappointed look, "Nothing about that Wilde fellow." He looked at Mildred waiting at the counter. "What can I do for you?"

She tried not to let her emotions show when she handed him her telegram. "Can you send this today?"

The machine started to click again. "Yeah, sure..." He turned around to see what was arriving, and without looking back at her said, "Just leave it on the counter."

She wanted to wait, to insist he send it, and felt put upon with how unprofessionally he conducted his business. But, as usual, she said nothing and left. She wound her way back out through the crowd that had gathered a few more stragglers. The last thing she heard was, "Hanging isn't good enough for the likes of them."

That comment sent her gut into a knotted tension as she made her way down the wooden walkway of the main street. She noticed how dull and devoid of life everything appeared. Dirt in the road was loose from the dry winter sending billows of dust following footsteps, tumbleweeds following horses. Buildings, in need of new paint, looked dreary. Even the women dressed in various shades of colors looked drab. She thought of Edra, her cousin, out at the ranch alone and her heart grew heavy. *What if…* It was futile to try to stop the replay of the telegraph office conversations.

She passed the sheriff's office where she noticed through the open door overweight Sheriff Matt Roper sitting at his desk with his feet up, stuffing a piece of pie into his mouth and talking to Deputy Jake Cummings. The minute Roper caught sight of Mildred he jumped up and lumbered out of his office.

"Mildred!" He wiped some crumbs from the side of his mouth onto his already dirty pant leg.

Mildred felt the tension in the back of her neck rise to the top of her skull. She turned around when she heard her name called and harsh footsteps banging on the planks approached her. "Yes, Matt." She moved a hand to the nape of her neck to rub a tender spot.

"Hey, Mildred. About that loan you authorized at the bank last fall…"

Mildred looked on, preoccupied by the throbbing behind her eyes.

"I reckon we'll be able to start making payments next month."

Mildred winced.

"You okay, Mildred?"

"Why yes," she lied. "Lot of commotion going on at the telegraph office this morning." She wasn't good at small talk but this was the only thing that came to her, which she regretted the minute she said it.

"Good thing they put that guy in prison. Tell you this, he's lucky he wasn't shot on the spot. Me? I know what I'd a done. Hang the…"

Mildred, preoccupied, heard jumbled words coming at her that made no sense.

"Two men together…" Matt's face flushed. "Not the thing for me to be talking about with a lady, Mildred. I better mind my manners."

Anxiety gripped her chest, making it difficult to get air in. "I better be getting on now. I have a sick horse I need to tend to."

"Yeah, well. Just wanted to thank you again for all your help. We'll be getting to those payments."

"Just pay when you can." She turned to walk away.

"Sure thing, thanks." Roper's voice trailed after her as he watched her walk down the street past the bank. When he was sure she was out of earshot, he walked to the door of his office and laughed to Jake, "Man, that's one ugly woman. To think I just called her a lady."

"More like a cow, a giant cow. Man, that's one tall giant cow," Jake laughed.

Town talk about Mildred centered on her plain appearance, a slightly prematurely receding hairline with some facial hair above her lip, muscles that showed through her dress sleeves like a man's through his shirt, and a height that towered over a lot of the men at close to six feet. She did not take a liking to dressing herself fashionably, instead finding comfort in simple attire that served a purpose for riding Lil and overseeing ranch work. Her looks, the way she dressed, her wealth, even her relationship with Edra brought her constant criticism. It mattered not that she was generous to a fault and helped support anyone in need when occasion arose nor that she forwent more than half of those she loaned money to when they failed to pay her back.

*

At the northeast corner of the block, business as usual was going on in Gus Spivey's General Store when Mildred entered and was instantly taken by the aroma of cinnamon. She moved past displays of tins of biscuits and jars of hard candies and approached where Gus was piling up bolts of fabrics next to the boxes of buttons, needles, threads, and other sewing items. One of the ends of the bolts came loose, sending a bin of nails, screws, latches, and other hardware flying to the floor.

"Damn it!" He placed the bolt of cloth on a shelf then turned to see Mildred behind him. The bowtie tightened around his neck.

15

"Apologies, Mildred. Didn't see you there. How can I help you?"

Gus had a kind face that suited him well. He was a pudgy man who wore circular glasses that were always slipping down his nose, and when he talked his stubby little finger would constantly have to readjust them to get the blur to disappear. He liked his work and catering to people in town and knew no enemies, for he went out of his way to be amicable. Whereas Satchel's telegraph office brought gossip into it freely, Gus's store rarely harbored more than a few sentences passed along from customers to him. He tended to curb things from getting out of hand, with rare exceptions (of which this day was one), and he was frazzled by all the commotion. But, like Mildred, it was his habit to keep his insides to himself.

Mildred took in the mess splattered over the floor. "Take a minute to clean that up so you don't go and hurt yourself. I'll just take a look around." She was glad she had a minute to catch her breath, to distract her attention from how she was feeling. She went to the display of canned goods, spices, and coffee. She took hold of a canister of tea, then walked over to take a look at the new crockery, pots and pans Gus must have received since her last visit to town.

A crowd began to gather around the noticeboard at the end of the aisle where Gus posted the latest news, including telegrams, for the town to read. When Mildred moved into range she heard the same commotion going on, mainly women chattering, that she had heard at the telegraph office just a short while before. She quickly moved back to where Gus was after he had all but cleaned up. She put the canister of tea and several other items she had chosen from the shelves down on the counter.

"I think I got it all now. Thanks for your patience, Mildred." Gus looked at her and then to the crowd. "That poor guy met a bad lot."

Mildred drew in a slow breath through her nostrils, noting what she thought was a tone of sympathy in Gus's voice.

"Will this be all for you, Mildred?"

"Yes." She hesitated a moment then decided to comment on why she came in.

"That horse medicine you ordered, the wrong one arrived."

"Oh no, I'm sorry, Mildred. I don't know how that could have happened."

The din of the crowd rose. "If that guy would've been churchgoing, he wouldn't have sunk to such evil!"

"Perversion!"

"It's a mockery of God. I tell you it's a slap in the face of the Lord."

Gus noticed Mildred's distraction. "They'll be going at it for weeks over this one." He was trying to say he was sorry that there wasn't much he could do about it and wished she didn't have to hear it.

Although Gus smiled at Mildred, it did nothing to calm the feeling of nausea rising in her belly. She paid for the items she'd gathered and made her way out of the store. The crowd's words rang in her mind: *churchgoing…violating the Lord…church…*along with surfacing images of her beloved deceased father Max. Even though she never understood or questioned the wisdom of her father's aversion to going to church, Mildred had worshiped him. Her mother Sadie had spent years pleading with her husband to go until, with utter hopelessness, she gave up and let him be. Although Mildred never cared for attending church, she did continue her mother's tradition of making generous annual contributions. Josie rumored that it must be hush money. While Max was alive there were whispers around town because he did not attend but no one dared say as much to his face. After his and Sadie's death, Josie Purdue stopped being careful with her talk, persecuting Mildred at every opportunity. While Mildred was generous in helping people financially when need arose, it did not stop them from joining Josie in the shunning, ridicule, and mean-spirited gossip. No one dare butt up against Josie's forceful personality to gain an understanding of why she had such a strong distaste for Mildred, which ran deeper than jealousy, nor did they chance her wrath by disagreeing.

As she left, Mildred noted that Josie was now at the public notice-board loudly voicing her opinion. "Homosexuality is officially illegal. We didn't need England to tell us it's a vile criminal act! Shooting is too good for him."

Even though Mildred knew Josie's comment wasn't directed at her, unlike earlier times when Josie accused her of being sinful for not attending church, she felt the sting. She had never worried about an escalation to something dangerous before, but after all she'd heard this morning, she was no longer sure. She knew Josie could no longer be ignored. As she rode back to her place soaked in sweat from worry, she tried to think of what she could do were things to get out of hand. When she passed the Whitmore's ranch, a couple of miles from her place, she had an idea. By the time she arrived home, it had percolated into a plan she was sure would work. It took her a couple of hours to convince Edra.

"Charity creates a multitude of sins." Oscar Wilde

2

While the town was still abuzz with the Wilde commotion, a singular room in Red River Pass was silent—a quiet that was interrupted by deep, growling, irregular breathing coming from Emma Milpass. She lay in a semi-comatose state, just days from death's door. Her husband Charley refused to accept the fact that Emma's cancer had spread to her brain. She would never return to answer his prayers. And he was not about to let her go.

Charley sat vigil at Emma's bedside, neglecting to bathe or feed himself. He washed away the sweat from her forehead and changed the rag of a diaper she wore even though it was barely soiled from the lack of fluids in her body. She was barely recognizable.

Just a few months back, they had been quite the couple, *the lookers*, he with his rugged handsome tanned face, blondish hair turning gray, angular nose and brown penetrating eyes, and she a natural beauty all her life. He was so worn from grief and worry he looked twice his age. He couldn't bear to watch her physical deterioration, part by part, each change representing a loss of the love of his life. It started back last winter when he noticed a yellow tinge in her eyes. It wasn't so much that he saw this change but how it made him feel, scared inside, that no matter how hard he tried to pretend it was nothing, deep down he knew differently. Week by week, what he never wanted to live through, his worst fears were reinforced as the changes screamed at him, *your wife is dying.*

While he tended to her every need, he neglected his own, forcing his brother-in-law Frank Whitmore to rally the town to help. "He needs us to go feed him," Frank told his wife Helene. "Town folk are starting to complain that body of his smells something awful. This has to stop or he'll be a mess on our hands when Emma's time comes." That was forty-eight hours before the Wilde telegram hit the town, shifting gossip away from Charley. Frank assembled close friends to bring meals and try to get Charley to take a break to bathe. The day after the Wilde news broke, Mildred offered to help. By joining in with the efforts to assist Charley, she wanted to create an impression of interest in him to divert any suspicion that might arise about her and Edra.

Doc Nichols made his way into the bedroom where Charley stood vigil. "It's a blessing it made its way to her brain," he said under his breath. Two weeks earlier when Emma started to slur her speech, he knew the cancer had migrated to her brain where it would continue to grow until she lapsed into a coma, a peaceful sleep into death.

"Nonsense! What the hell are you talking about? What damn kind of blessing is that!" Charley said, without turning around to face the doctor.

"She's peaceful, Charley. It's better than medicine. She'll just sleep now till…"

Charley stood, kicking his chair back. "I think you'd better be going. I can see we don't need any of your help here!" he screamed. "Blessing, my ass!"

Nichols put a hand on Charley's shoulder. "She's out of her misery. Be thankful for that."

Charley pulled back. "I don't want her to be peaceful. I want her to be alive! Like it was. Like it was." He broke down in tears.

"Go on, Charley. Let it out."

Charley sank back into the chair, put his head down on Emma's chest, and let out the grief that could not find its way to daylight while she was still conscious. Nichols felt Charley tense when he put a hand on his back.

"If you was a real doctor, you could save her," Charley moaned, referring to the fact that Nichols lacked medical schooling. The only professional training he had was apprenticing with a doctor in Saint Louis where he grew up.

Nichols felt a familiar sorrow that his parents could not afford to properly educate him. He knew Charley was talking out of his grief. "Try and get a little rest now. I'll be back later."

*

The bell hanging over the front door clanged, waking Charley from a deep sleep. Disoriented, he looked around to get his bearings, when he noticed Emma breathing very shallowly. He reached over to touch her limp hand with absolutely no response from her. The bell clanged again. "Go away!" he screamed.

"Charley, I brought you some food."

A rush of anger welled up inside him. "Why can't you just leave me alone? Stay away! I don't want none of your food!"

Emma did not stir.

Mildred entered Charley's living room and set down a tray with a pot of stew of meat, onions, carrots, potatoes and gravy. In a small tin were freshly baked biscuits soaked in melted butter. "I'll bring a plate in to you," she called.

Exasperated, Charley turned away from Emma. "Just leave it there and go!"

Mildred walked to the partially open door. "I'm not leaving till you come out and eat some. How are you going to take care of Emma if you lose your strength? I'm staying right here, Charley Mil…"

The bedroom door banged open, knocking Mildred's left side. "Ouch." She stepped back.

"If you'd have left when I asked you to, you wouldn't be in my way. Now get."

Mildred absorbed how worn he looked: sullen face, disheveled clothes, and the foul odor of his body. She could not tell if his brown eyes were red from lack of sleep or crying and almost felt sorry for him. She stepped back, letting him pass. "Here. I brought you some stew and biscuits. Eat and I'll leave." She rubbed the sore spot where the door had jammed into her.

Charley walked to the food without comment and lifted the stew pot lid, then slammed it down. "I'm not hungry. Go on now, Mildred, get!"

"I'm going nowhere till you stop acting like a child and sit down and eat a bit." She put her hands on her hips and gave him a look that said she meant business.

"You folks coming over here are a pain in the butt. Can't nobody be left alone?" He scooped a spoonful of stew and took a swallow. "There."

"That's a good start. If you're that antsy to get rid of me, then eat some more and I'll leave." She pulled a chair to the table and motioned for him to sit down, patting the chair next to hers.

He sat, spooned out some stew, and began to eat while Mildred sat silently looking around. She noticed clothes thrown about over the couch in his living room, dirty dishes piled up in the kitchen, dust everywhere, cobwebs on a lamp, and to her disgust, a few rat droppings. The silence was suddenly interrupted by loud snoring noises coming from the bedroom. "Oh poor Emma," Mildred whispered.

Charley pushed his chair back, dropping his spoon to the floor, and ran to his wife. Mildred tidied the place before leaving. He never noticed the doorbell clanging as she made her way out.

"What's happening to you?" Charley took Emma's ashen face in his hands. As he gazed at her, the last hint of pink blotches left her cheeks. Her breathing grew louder and more labored until the snoring was barely audible. Instinctively, he put the side of his head right next to her mouth. He felt his heart pounding while the last faint trace of air from her lungs gently grazed his face. When there was nothing warm hitting his cheek, panic set in. He grabbed her torso and shook her while he screamed, "No! No! No! Don't leave me! Emma!"

*

Mildred was irritated as she rode back to her ranch. "How are we ever going to work this out, Lil?" she mumbled to her painted horse. "That man is not making this easy."

She was annoyed with herself that she decided to help Charley but did not know what else to do. She hated drawing attention to herself and being subjected to ridicule. *She looks and acts like a man. Look at that receding hairline; she's going bald. She's a fat pig.* Even worse, she resented talk of her cousin, Edra. *What a hermit. She'll never get over what happened to her.* This she could not forgive. She knew that in devising her plan she had to swallow all this and come across as credibly as she could in showing an interest in Charley. Compared to the alternative, of doing nothing and being found out, it was a small price to pay.

Lil jerked and sped forward, snapping Mildred's attention from her frustration.

"Whoa, girl. Take it easy."

Lil had, on her own, turned up the dirt road of the ranch through the double row of pinyon pines that had been planted by Mildred's father to give privacy to the Dunlap's homestead. Clouds of dust rose to the height of the buggy seat, and Mildred wondered what was beneath all that flying dirt. It had only been two days since she had come across a rattlesnake den in a gully, just feet from where Lil was trotting. She wondered if Lil remembered this, and the other time when a rattler grabbed onto Chessie, the family's blue merle Australian Shepherd. Lil had watched that dog go down in a painful squirming death. Mildred was so distraught over the loss that she refused to get another dog. Edra, traumatized from watching it also, refused to walk anywhere near the site for weeks. Mildred reached to feel the rifle at her side and was glad that she had learned to sharp-shoot at an early age, along with Edra. *It's for protection, girls,* she recalled her father telling her and Edra while he trained them to do everything young men could do, so that they would be able to fend for themselves when the time came.

Mildred saw a dim light coming from the master bedroom window as she climbed out of the buggy and tied Lil to the hitching post outside the front door. Once inside her place, she saw a freshly baked apple pie on the dining room table, which quelled the aggravation caused by Charley's stubbornness.

"Hey Edra, you there?" she called to the bedroom.

"What took you so long? That pie is getting cold," Edra called out as she entered the living room.

Mildred saw Edra's beautiful face and shiny brown hair, dark with natural curls that fell from the tie that held it back off her neck, contrasting with her radiant green eyes. Edra's shapely figure was shown well in her Sears & Roebuck gingham dress and the simple brown lace-up shoes. "I'm glad this day's over." Mildred moved closer to her.

"Come, sit down. Let's have some pie and you can tell me about it."

"Selfishness is not living as one wishes to live,
it is asking others to live as one wishes to live."

OSCAR WILDE

3

Swirls of dusty heat rose to meet Helene Whitmore's cool glass of brewed sage flower as she sat outside in the setting sun. She delighted in the mildly bitter flavor when mixed with a little honey, which helped to quiet her nerves. Doc Nichols told her, "The Indians have been using sage flower as medicine for decades, to calm and relax…" She needed something to help her dark moods and preferred this to hard liquor. First time booze touched her lips at the age of twelve when she started womanhood, it was from drool spilling from her father's mouth as he was having his way with her. He didn't go after her because of how she looked; she was a plain thin girl, with no outstanding features. She never understood why it happened and endured years of humiliation, hiding at home to avoid others seeing her bruises, without the protection of her mother and siblings who were also victims. As Helene aged, so did her father's violence so that by the time she was fifteen, she married the first man who showed an interest in her. Frank, also ordinary in countenance, was more interested in work than physicality.

The Whitmore children were asleep, and while the faint trace of daylight lingered, Frank Whitmore made his way to the barn to check on one of his pregnant cows. Helene welcomed the time alone, which she knew would end once Emma died.

Emma, very close to her brother Frank, begged him to take care of Charley when her time came. "I know he's strong-willed, Frank. I know it, but you have to promise me. I don't have long," she had cried to her brother. "He's a stubborn man. Keeps everything in till he's ready to explode. You got to promise me, on your strongest word." Frank had taken his sister's hand and nodded his agreement.

As the sun was setting, stealing away the last moments of daylight, Frank returned. "The heifer's holding her own. But if the other one don't spring soon, we might be in trouble. You going to head out to check on Emma now?"

Helene couldn't ignore his parched wrinkled face from years of working the field, prematurely graying hair, slouched posture, and baggy coveralls. "This is really getting to you."

"Charley's a mess." He paused and wiped the sweat from his brow with the back of his hand. "We'll work it out. You tell my sister I can't make it tonight."

"I don't think we need to be worrying about telling Emma anything. She won't know the difference." Helene sipped her drink.

He gave her a disgusted look. "You tell her!"

She shrunk back into herself. "Okay, settle down. I didn't mean nothing by that."

"If the calf come out alright, I'll make it there tomorrow."

*

When Helene arrived, she found Charley in the bedroom with Emma. It took her a moment to understand what was happening. "Oh dear Lord!"

Charley's head was on Emma's lifeless chest, his arms around her cold limbs, the only motion his sobbing.

"I'll be with you soon, my Emma!" he cried. Charley lifted his head and screamed at the ceiling, "Take me! Take me now!"

*

As Mildred soaked in a hot tub that Edra had filled for her behind a partition next to the kitchen, she heard a knock at the door. "What the… Who's coming at this hour? Edra! Someone's at the door!"

Edra moved swiftly, returning a moment later to find Mildred out of the tub and wrapped in her robe. "What's going on?"

"It's Frank. He's asking if you can go to his place…"

"At this hour? I'm not going back out…"

"Emma died. He wants you to watch his children." Edra relayed that Charley's neighbor rode out to tell Frank. "Said Helene's a mess and wouldn't leave him alone."

Mildred was taken aback. "I didn't expect this so soon. Good thing I got over there today…" She hesitated to get her wits about her. "This is going to speed things up…"

"You mean the plan?" asked Edra.

"Yes. Tell Frank I'll be there in about twenty minutes." Mildred wondered about Helene's reaction.

After Mildred left, Edra made use of the still-warm bath water to ease the tension she was feeling since agreeing to go along with Mildred's idea. She did not see how the Wilde commotion would change things between them and tried to get Mildred to see her point of view, to no avail. Although it did not sit right with Edra, Mildred had been so sure, strong in her opinion that the way people were talking would impact their lives were any suspicions to form. It was the fear she sensed in Mildred that finally cinched the deal for her and she resigned herself to go along with it. She was no stranger to stress; trauma held in her cells from her brutal rape. A good soaking in the bath would help relieve her knotted muscles. She got into the water, closed her eyes and drifted back.

On a day when thirteen-year-old Mildred had gone into town with her father, her nine-year-old cousin Edra was left at home with Mildred's mother, to get over a cough. While Sadie was in the kitchen preparing supper, Edra snuck out to go to the meadow behind the Dunlap house. She loved to rest under a huge single-leaf pinyon pine tree that grew next to a bristlecone pine, their branches intertwining. In her place of sanctuary she would watch mountain bluebirds, hummingbirds, osprey, and once to her excitement, a bald eagle. She enjoyed the feel and texture of the sandstones between her fingers. It was under these trees that she met Swifty, the name she gave to a desert tortoise.

Edra knelt to the ground and reclined in a comfortable position. She looked up at the trees shading her while the exhaustion of the fever took her to sleep. She could not remember how long her eyes were closed before she was awakened by loud laughter.

"Why lookie here." The itinerant was unkempt and smelled foul.

Edra, dazed, tried to sit up. The man pushed her down with a foot to her chest, and jumped astride her, lowering his body on top of hers.

"My, you is a beauty. You been waiting here for me, darling?" He ripped at her blouse with one hand and held her firm with the other, lifted her skirt, and entered into areas she never knew could receive so much pain.

The last thing Edra remembered, before losing consciousness, was the man's face moving in on hers, his acrid breath.

It was Mildred who found her and was there for her, day and night, combing her hair, rubbing her back, filling her tub, bringing her meals, and after many months coaxing her back outside to return to the place that had once given her so much joy, now a place she feared.

The cooling water in the tub sent a shiver up her spine as she continued to remember. In the weeks that followed, it was Mildred's insistence then, just as now over the Wilde turbulence, that spoke to her. *Mildred holding out a hand to her and saying, "Let's take a walk. You need to face this. It's for your own healing."*

"Not today, Mil. I will another time. I promise."

"You've promised me that many times. Come on. I'll be at your side."

Edra broke out in a sweat when Mildred grabbed hold of her hand. She refused to move. "I can't."

Mildred tightened her grip. She then put her other hand in the pocket of the dress she was wearing and grabbed hold of the derringer nestled in there. When she pulled it out she said, "You're safe. No one is ever going to hurt you again. Do you hear me? I'll kill any bastard who puts a hand on you!"

Edra felt the weight of her legs start to move and with a racing heart followed slightly behind Mildred at a slow pace. When the trees came into view Edra stopped. "I can't go any further."

Mildred squeezed her hand and in a comforting tone said, "We're almost there. You're okay. You're going to be okay. Trust me."

Edra continued to move along with Mildred. Once upon the place where the trees intertwined, Mildred caught sight of Swifty coming out of a nearby bush. "Well, look who's coming."

Edra felt a startle. "What!"

Mildred pointed to where the tortoise was creeping along a couple of feet away. "Probably take him another two days to get to us. I bet he missed you."

The memory of the conversation shifting to Swifty, and how Mildred tried to cheer her up, made Edra smile. She got out of the cold water and dried herself. She thought about Mildred's urgency when describing the plan and wondered if it could work. Mildred was sure that if she showed interest in Charley by bringing food to him at Emma's bedside, it would start the gossip going. She would continue to show interest in Charley until he rejected her.

"Suffering is one very long moment.
We cannot divide it into seasons." OSCAR WILDE

4

In the weeks that followed Emma's death, the people in town kept a vigil on Charley. Shifts were mustered to bring food and offer comfort. The melodrama in town was fueled by a rumor Josie started that Charley was suicidal. Mildred continued to bring him food. She could not stomach his histrionics but knew that she had to endure them. "I'm going to take Mabel Whitmore along with me today," she told Edra.

"You can't take a four-year-old around Charley. It'll scare her."

"Charley's not going to do anything to upset his own niece."

"I don't know about that. That man seems out of control," Edra insisted.

Mildred softened her voice. "Trust me."

The buggy ride to Charley's place consisted of an endless stream of "What's that?" with Mabel pointing at everything her eyes set sight on and getting under Mildred's skin something awful. It was all she could do to maintain her composure. She resisted fending off Mabel's barrage. "Listen here, honey," Mildred hesitated, wondering if her tone was too stern. "Your Uncle Charley has been feeling a little sad lately so we're going to play a game with him."

"A game! What game? I like games!"

"We're going to play, let's make Uncle Charley smile and laugh."

She felt silly. This was out of character for her but she wanted to deflect attention off her when they arrived, and nothing else came to mind.

"How do we play that? I never heard of that game. Tell me, Mildred."

"Well, you see honey…"

Mabel interrupted, "Tell me! Tell me!"

Mildred's grip tightened on the reins. "I'm trying. Settle down there a minute."

Mabel squirmed in her seat. "I'm waiting!"

"When we get there…"

"Yes, tell me!"

"When we get there…" She drew a slow breath. "You just tell your uncle all the things that make you laugh."

"When my feet get tickled," Mabel chuckled.

"There you go. Let's see how many things we can think of. Whoever makes him laugh the most is the winner."

"When daddy tickles me on my sides."

The view of town came into sight across the open dry desert, with a few tumbleweeds flying around the scattered pinyons. The warmth of the sun felt good, relieving some of the tension Mildred was feeling about visiting Charley again.

"Yes, yes." Mildred turned left at the corner by Gus Spivey's General Store. "Almost there. Just be a minute now."

When Mabel saw Charley's place, she bounced with excitement. "Uncle Charley!" she screamed. "Uncle Charley, we come to play!" She ran to the front door.

"What's all that commotion?" Charley asked Harry Peterson, sitting vigil at the side of his bed. "Can't you people just go and let me be?" He heard another scream coming from his front porch. "Stop all that racket!" he yelled.

"Uncle Charley!"

"That sounds like a child." Charley paused. "Sounds like Mabel," he said to Harry.

When Harry left Charley to get the door, Mabel burst in, nearly knocking him over.

"It is you, Mabel. Who in God's name brought you here?"

"Uncle Charley." Mabel threw herself on the bed next to him. "Mildred brought me to play with you." Mabel was not fazed by the fact that Charley looked old and worn with his hair in need of cutting, nor did she notice his dull brown eyes surrounded by newly formed wrinkles.

"Mildred? What the hell…"

"You said a bad word," admonished Mabel. "My mom told me never to say a bad…"

That calmed him. "Okay, young lady." Emma Milpass had loved her niece Mabel, a fact that was not forgotten by Charley. He also had a soft spot for her. "Mabel, your Uncle Charley here isn't feeling well. Go and get Mildred to take you home."

Mabel pulled a face and pouted, "I don't want to leave."

When Mildred approached the bedroom door, Charley shot her a look. "Mildred, you need to take Mabel back home. This is no place for my little niece to be."

"I'm not going!" Mabel responded vehemently.

"Calm down now, Mabel," Charley urged.

"Charley, why don't you just get on up and we'll all have a little snack together. Mabel has something in store for you after that."

"Come on, Uncle Charley." Mabel tugged at his arm until he got up. "Do you have any cookies?"

Charley begrudgingly moved to the kitchen with Mabel. "I don't know what we got here," he mumbled, as Harry signaled to Mildred that he was leaving.

"I'm hungry," Mabel whined. "Here." She opened a cabinet where Emma had kept cookies and candy for the kids who visited them and pulled out a tin of stale cookies.

"How about some tea?" Mildred suggested to Charley as she picked the kettle up off the stove, filled it with water, and started a fire.

"We gonna play a game with you, Uncle Charley," Mabel said, biting down on a hard chocolate-chip cookie.

Charley surrendered to Mabel's exuberance. He watched while she jumped up and down in excitement and took notice of the scrapes on her banged-up knees. "How'd you get all those bruises?" he asked.

"Cranky."

Cranky, the Whitmore's yellow-haired mutt, was a handful. As a puppy, he had unbounded energy and was always getting into mischief chewing anything he could get in his mouth. His name was Yellow Dog until he tore Mabel's favorite hand-sewn cotton doll to shreds. Mabel was inconsolable till Helene promised to sew another one that very same day. *"He's just being cranky,"* Helene told Mabel while she patched together a new doll.

"Cranky, Cranky, Cranky," Mabel squealed at him.

That name stayed.

Charley looked down at his niece. "What's Cranky been into now? Come here and let me have a look..."

Mildred noticed that Charley seemed to be perking up.

"That's some dog you have there, little missy." Charley patted Mabel's head. "He still running with two balls in his mouth?"

"He can do three now, Uncle Charley."

"Three balls. Well! How about that?" Charley smiled.

Mabel burst forth with stories about her play with Cranky while Mildred sat by and took it in. They stayed until Sam Larue came to relieve Mildred's watch. After taking them to her buggy, he returned to find Charley heating up water for a bath. "I won't be needing you here, Sam."

"I don't know."

Charley smiled. "What does this look like to you, Sam? I'm gonna have myself a bath. Then when I clean myself up, this place here needs some help. Go on now. Go home to your family. I'll be okay." He saw Sam's hesitancy and continued, "Don't be worrying. It's just gonna take time."

"You sure?" Sam needed to reassure himself.

When Charley responded, he was convinced it'd be okay to leave.

"One should absorb the color of life." OSCAR WILDE

5

It had been on Edra's twelfth birthday, three years after she was raped, that things forever changed between the two girls. The rape that had been a curse up until then would transform into a dark blessing. When the search party came back empty-handed, people understood why Edra felt unsafe venturing outside the ranch. For Edra, who was becoming a beautiful young lady, it became the accepted excuse for lack of interest in socializing. Mildred did not need a reason. No one paid attention to why she had no friends and spent her time with the ranch animals and her traumatized cousin. Her homely, overly tall, and masculine appearance at a young age was fodder for heckling. Through the years, town folk, particularly mean-spirited Josie and her friends, did not let up or spare her when she was in earshot. *She's ugly. No one will ever take to her. Good thing she has her cousin...no one else would want her.*

Mildred had just finished her chores and gone to the kitchen to help with birthday preparations when Edra called her back to the living room. "It's warm." The blistering heat made Edra feel lethargic. "Let's go for a swim in Walker Lake."

"I have to help mamma with your cake. You go on."

Edra pouted, "It's my birthday. I'm not going if you don't." She went to the kitchen, where Sadie was pouring baking ingredients into a bowl, and returned to Mildred a moment later. "Mamma told me it's okay for you to go."

"Edra," said Mildred, noting there was still plenty of daylight left, "you're going to wear me out."

Edra's excitement rose. "Let's go."

"Wait a sec. Let me get my things."

Edra felt warm inside. Her nipples hardened like they did when it was cold outside, and a sensation crept into her body that she had only recently experienced, way down deep inside. A yearning burst up her spine when Mildred returned and grabbed her arm to get going.

The air cooled as they approached an isolated area of trees at the lakeside. "Here's a good spot." Mildred looked over to Edra for agreement.

"I forgot to bring my suit," Edra lied.

"You forgot your suit?"

"I don't need a swimsuit. I'm going in naked."

"What?"

"No one ever comes out this way. I'm not getting my clothes wet. It's hot." She unbuttoned the back of her dress, disrobed, and ran to the water.

Mildred smiled inside, feeling a sense of satisfaction over how much Edra had changed since the time when she was violated. At first it was very slow going, an incredible effort to even get her to mention the incident, but with time and nurturing Mildred helped her return to where it happened. After that, Edra learned to trust and open to Mildred, to become playful again, and even take risks, like today, that she hadn't since being traumatized. She was returning to herself and as she recovered, their affection grew.

"I don't know what I am going to do with you," Mildred muttered to herself as she got out of her skirt and blouse, and folded them neatly. She took off her undergarments and put on her swimsuit, wrapped herself in a large towel, and then made her way down to the water.

"This feels great!" Edra screamed and splashed, sending ripples right up to Mildred's legs, now knee-deep.

Edra floated over to Mildred as she made her way deeper into the water. She moved closer and let her arms slide down over Mildred's buttocks.

"Don't pull me under like that," Mildred said, as she broke loose. She turned onto her back and floated around feeling the coolness of the water under her as the sun baked hot on her face.

Edra paddled about keeping her full attention on Mildred's body, the curves of her fully formed breasts showing through the thickness of the swimsuit that went all the way to her knees. As Edra watched, she felt the stirrings returning, warming her insides in the coolness of the water. She drifted closer and placed a hand on Mildred's belly.

"Hey, watch out. You'll drown me," Mildred laughed.

"Mildred." Edra put her arms around Mildred's waist and drew her close. "I love you."

Mildred backstroked away, kicking water to stay afloat. "The feeling is mutual. Now watch it."

Edra trod water. "I think I have different feelings than we have talked about before." She paddled toward Mildred. "Let's get out." Edra had first sensed her affinity for Mildred's body, a woman's body, a couple of years earlier when she got excited entertaining thoughts of them together, without clothes on. When she turned eleven, the attraction grew, along with the awareness that she didn't feel the same preference toward a man's body. She knew what she wanted, what she needed, and what sat right in her skin.

Mildred didn't know what to make of Edra's comment. "I won't be much longer. It's so nice here." She moved her arms to stay afloat. "I'll just be a little bit."

Edra went ashore and wrapped herself in a towel. While she sat and watched Mildred, feelings inside her screamed for attention. She wanted to explore what was happening. She yearned to be touched in places that she had only, until now, gone to by herself; places where hair was starting to appear, where tingling erupted when she moved her hands and rubbed herself near the folds of skin and moistness. She wanted to experience what it would be like to be naked and touched by the only person alive she felt safe with and trusted completely. Edra let the towel fall to her waist as Mildred approached.

"Cover yourself up," Mildred admonished.

"Come here. I need to talk to you." Edra made no motion toward her towel.

Mildred moved to cover her with the towel that she was holding. Edra resisted.

"What's gotten into you?" asked Mildred.

Edra rose, letting the towel fall to the ground. "Mildred." She stretched out her arms.

"Edra. Stop that."

"I'll die if you don't touch me." She moved her face close to Mildred's and placed her lips gently upon her cousin's. "Please, I love you."

Mildred pulled away. "This is wrong." The words belied how she felt. She was bursting inside.

"How can my loving you be wrong? Please." Edra gently moved back to Mildred.

"What if someone comes…"

"No one ever comes here."

✻

Max Dunlap had seen this attraction forming between the girls before they discovered it together. He had recognized the same kind of relating that he noticed when his older brother Ben was around the neighbor's boy, Jessie Buckstorm, back in Ohio. Max had known that he would have to take care of his daughter and niece in ways they would never understand until they were older. He had his wife school them at the ranch. He took them out daily and taught them how to shoot guns and rifles and tend to ranch business. He saw the seeds that were planted well before the bloom, and he dedicated his life to taking care to protect what the girls would grow into.

"The secret of life is to appreciate the pleasure of being terribly, terribly deceived." Oscar Wilde

6

The closest house to the Dunlap's ranch was the Whitmore's, a couple of miles away, on the other side of a hill. Through the years Frank Whitmore had shown up with questions about things that needed repair or issues involving rent payments, so it was not unusual that he appeared asking to see Mildred, since it was she who dealt with her tenants. When Frank discovered that Edra was home alone, he left without leaving a message.

"Frank came by," she said to Mildred later.

"What did he want?"

"Didn't say," Edna replied as she removed a steeping tea ball from a pot of tea and poured herself a cup. "Want one?"

"No. He just showed up here then left? That's not like him."

"You going over there?" Edra took a sip of tea.

"No, just leave it. If he needs something he'll come back."

"So how did it go with Charley? What happened with Mabel?"

"I told you not to worry, didn't I?"

"Well?"

Mildred relayed the events that had occurred at Charley's.

Edra listened and felt uneasy. It was the same disquiet she experienced when Mildred initially brought up the plan. She didn't like being talked into something on the fly, without time to think things through and weigh all the possibilities, but Mildred convinced her that with all the hatred flying about they needed to be proactive. "I don't know about all this…I think we rushed…" Something stuck in her craw that she was unable to put her finger on.

"Don't worry. Everything's working out just fine."

"I don't know, Mil. My gut is telling me different." She hesitated before asking, "Maybe we should think this over?"

"There's nothing to rethink. We've set it in motion and it'll work. There's no other way or we'd have thought of it." Mildred saw how distressed Edra was. "You're getting all worked up over nothing. You know the rant Josie goes on over our not going to church…" She went on to remind Edra about all they'd heard from their ranch hand Ben through the years, about accusations on how they lived in sin because they didn't go to church. "If Josie was up in arms about that, can you imagine what she'd do if she suspected us…"

"Why's Josie targeting you? Surely we're not the only ones who don't go."

"I don't know why she has a bee in her bonnet over me. Some things you can't explain."

"I hope you're right about all this."

That night Edra tossed and turned in a fitful sleep, keeping Mildred awake. What she couldn't make sense of that was bothering her from earlier in the day came to her in a screaming nightmare. "The bed!"

"Edra," Mildred whispered to calm her.

"Huh," she mumbled back.

"You're having a bad dream. Come here." Mildred pulled Edra into her arms.

"Mil…" Edra, still half-asleep, nuzzled into Mildred's chest. "I'm afraid."

"Shhhhhhh. It's going to be okay. Try to get back to sleep." Mildred stroked her back till she slept again. Next morning, upon waking Mildred said to her, "You had a rough night…you screamed about a bed in the middle of the night."

"I had a nightmare. I just can't get my mind off…" Edra was reluctant to bring up what she dreamt.

"Did you want to say something else?"

"Not really."

"You sure?"

"There is one thing…" She burst into tears. "Oh God. What if someone comes in and sees the bed. I think we should put another one back in the den."

Mildred sat up straight, tensed, and spoke with a command. "That's what your dream was about?"

"Yes."

"That is never going to happen. Rest assured. Never!"

"We can't predict…what if something does happen…we're not prepared."

"Edra. No way in hell. Our home is where I draw the line. We've been safe and we'll continue to be safe."

"How can you be so sure?" Edra wiped her eyes.

"As sure as I am that I love you, that's how sure I am. I refuse to even entertain…"

"I'm sorry but I…"

"You've nothing to be sorry about. You've done nothing wrong, Edra. You just need to calm down and trust me a little more. I've thought this all through. All we're doing is setting up appearances and so far everything is working out just like I hoped. Once people get the notion I like Charley, we've accomplished what we wanted to. Won't be long after that he rejects me."

"I hope you're right."

"You know I am. You just need to calm down."

Edra felt ashamed she brought it up. "I'll try."

Mildred put a hand through Edra's hair and softened her tone. "That's my girl. That's all I ask of you. Just try to keep perspective." She made a motion to get out of bed then turned back to Edra. "Let's take the horses out today. Some fresh air will do us good."

"I thought you had some things to do with Ben."

"I should be done by midday."

"Okay."

Mildred finished her work by three in the afternoon and the women saddled up their horses, Mildred on Lil with Edra on Slim. They rode to a cool spot near a stream with running water by several full-grown pinyon trees. Edra halted Slim. "Let's tie them up here."

"It's a relief to get out." Mildred dismounted from Lil and pulled a wool blanket out of her saddlebag. She was relieved to see that the rash on Lil's side was healing. She recalled the day when she went in to town to order the medicine for Lil, and all the unanticipated events that set in motion the fear-driven plan that threatened irrevocably to disrupt their lives. Mildred had doubts but didn't dare share them with Edra and fuel her anxiety even more. She had to keep a check on what she was feeling, continue to be positive, be the strong one, and believe in her conviction that Charley would never show an interest. She knew that anything anyone had to say about her moves on him would be far less painful than the alternative. She would endure whatever she had to, to protect Edra and their relationship.

As Edra helped lay out the blanket, Mildred watched her move, the grace as she sat and stretched her arms upward to the cumulus clouds drifting by, and then reclined to take in the deep blue sky and the intensity of the sun. A bird sounded its presence as it chased a few of the remaining clouds on their way to another dance. The trees cast a welcoming shade as a place to rest. Edra's radiant green eyes softened into a sleepy haze as her lids gently closed, her full lips parted, and a sweet soft sound of peaceful breathing filled the air. Mildred gently stroked the sunlit hair cascading down Edra's back. She was overwhelmed with a sense of loving peace, that all was right with the world when they were together. This was short-lived before the doubts resurfaced. She hated the duplicity of her plan that went against her moral fiber. She hated all the years of having to misrepresent who she was and their relationship.

Edra looked so vulnerable, arms wide open inviting in what may come, so different from her protective guarding when around others. It

41

took her years to open to Mildred and learn to trust again. She loved and trusted no other human being. Mildred hated having to pretend to protect her but worse she feared the futility of doing nothing. She had to reassure her. A breeze picked up, awakening Edra. She sat up then stretched. "I needed that." She felt a chill. "It's cooling down."

Mildred noticed that the sun had dropped toward the horizon.

Edra stretched her arms. "We better get going back."

"Just a minute," Mildred hesitated, "taking the ride, just being here brought me some perspective."

"What?" Edra was still groggy.

"I don't want you to lose any more sleep. Everything's going to work out..."

Edra reached for her sweater. "I don't know... Something still doesn't feel right."

"Can't let our minds take over and sabotage what we worked out. I know it's going to work."

"What if it backfires?" Edra questioned.

"How? There's no way."

"What if Charley takes a liking to you?"

Mildred laughed. "There's no way in hell Charley is ever going to take a liking to me."

"I don't know..."

"Edra, you're so naive," laughed Mildred.

"You're making fun of me?"

"No, I'm not. Come on Edra, look at me." She waved a hand over the length of her body, patted her protruding belly, and pulled her receding hairline back.

"Stop messing around. This is serious. What if Charley sees you the way I do?"

"Never going to happen."

"How can you be so sure?" Edra looked worried.

"I won't let this get out of hand. How many times have we been over this? Look at the facts. They speak for themselves. Charley is just coming out of his loss with Emma. They were the couple of the town and nobody's ever shown an interest in me."

"I have."

"You know what I mean. I'm not someone a man would be interested in."

Edra was about to say something else then hesitated. "I hope you're right."

When the women arrived home there was a note attached to their front door. "What's that?" asked Edra.

"From Ben. He stopped by while we were out to have a look at the barn."

"And?"

"He'll go over it with me tomorrow when he's here."

*

Ben Thorndike was a loyal hand on the Dunlap's ranch under Mildred's parents. While Max and Sadie were alive, he helped with the cattle, did any number of odd jobs, and oversaw construction projects that the ranch needed. He continued on with the same chores with the exception of tending to the cattle, which Mildred sold off after her parents died. He was a closed-mouth employee with no delusions about how important his job was. He had a good thing going working for the wealthiest woman in Red River Pass. He would never let his wife Rose forget their good fortune when economic times turned bad and Mildred financed many of the townspeople to sustain them through the long hard winters. She steered clear of the local gossipers' dirt at Ben's urging and avoided giving input, but had an ear to the ground when shopping in town. The women tried to pump her for gossip but she knew better, with the constant reminder from Ben who told her on numerous occasions, "Don't be asking what is none of your business and don't be talking about Mildred to any of those ladies, who have nothing better to do with their time than bang their lips together in other people's lives. That's nothing but trouble, Rose. Do you hear me?" Despite all this, Rose never hesitated to pass along what she heard in town to Ben. He'd had an earful of late about Mildred's helping Charley.

"Morning, Mildred," Ben said as he stepped onto the porch where Mildred was drinking a cup of tea.

"Ben."

"I took a look at the barn yesterday and wrote up here what we need to do."

"And?"

"The rain last winter took its toll. There's an awful lot of wood rot. My best guess is we're going to have to replace the entire siding all the way down to the piers supporting the structure, which could cost a small fortune in supplies and labor."

Ben had the authority to tend to regular ranch business but this was beyond his working budget and he needed permission to get estimates and go ahead with repairs.

"Let's take a look."

Edra watched through the front window as they walked to the barn. She closed the curtain and sat down in a chair by the window. She had been preoccupied for the past two days with a sick feeling accompanying thoughts that would not quit. She recalled Mildred saying to her on more than one occasion, "I am a spinster who no one in their right mind would be interested in." But Edra knew how she felt and what a wonderful woman Mildred was, selflessly helping others in the face of ridicule and ingratitude. If she loved her, then it was not out of the question that someone else might feel the same. She could not bear to lose her and felt threatened by what might happen if their plan backfired. Mildred's continued attempts to reassure her did not alleviate the niggling feeling in her gut that would not let her rest.

Mildred returned and found Edra deep in thought. "We have quite a project on the barn."

Edra didn't respond.

"Also got some encouraging news from Ben. Seems that Rose overheard some of the women talking about Charley doing better. Said he ran into Frank who mentioned that Charley was grateful for me bringing over little Mabel."

Edra caught the tail end of what Mildred was saying. "What?"

"We were right about Josie. That woman can't keep her mouth shut."

Half paying attention, Edra asked, "What are you talking about?"

"It's Josie keeping the stir up about that Wilde fellow. She is the one we need to watch out for...and that tea sisterhood she hangs around with. Turns my stomach they have nothing better to do with their lives than look for the next life they can ruin. Vicious. We just have to be sure to fill her head with what we want in it. Seems that our plan is working."

"What do you mean?"

"Josie mentioned to her gaggle of frenzied followers that Charley is happy I came to visit."

"Ben told you that?" She anxiously continued, "Charley's happy..."

Mildred caught Edra's response, like an infection in her chest, tightening her airway. "Hey now, don't be giving any thought to anything Josie says. All we've got to be concerned with is planting the idea in her head that I like Charley. That'll take care of the rest of the town," Mildred laughed.

"I don't see what's so funny...what if he really is happy? What if he's starting to like you?"

"It's never going to happen. I've never been surer of ..." She caught herself in this exaggeration that was an obvious attempt to appease Edra. "You weren't there when I heard what people were saying. Not so much the words but the vengeance in their voices. They wanted blood. Josie is the worst of them." Her face flushed. "If she ever gets wind...if anyone does...it'd be no better than what the Parker boys did. Those little brats...running those good folk out of town. Not to mention the suicide. Next time it could be worse." She was getting worked up and knew she had to calm herself. "There's no easy answer, Edra. We need to keep the focus on why we're doing it and not run off into something that's not...that's never going to happen as far as Charley is concerned. I won't let it."

Edra's heart sank. "And if it does?"

"I won't let it." Mildred moved closer to Edra. "Please trust in my love for you."

She knew Mildred was right. Most of the small-minded people in town would give an eyetooth to see Mildred ruined. There was a lot of jealousy and hostility over Mildred being wealthy and controlling the purse strings in the community. She was already a target and Edra knew that what Mildred feared was that the story the town conjured up about them, that she was too traumatized and Mildred too homely to be in a relationship with a man, would not hold water were anyone to suspect them. This was something neither of them ever wanted to face.

"The plan is the only solution." Mildred looked intently at Edra. "If you can think of something better, I'm all ears."

"You know I can't."

"Then stop worrying."

*

Helene was relieved that she had managed to talk Frank into going over to the Dunlap's ranch to see Mildred. It took some doing to get her point across. She had her own plan in mind, to hook Charley up with Mildred, which might give her a chance of getting her hands on some of Mildred's money.

"I can't manage the kids and Charley. You've got your hands full here. What's the harm if they spend time together? Ease it up for us."

"Helene, you better not be up to any trouble. Mildred's been good to us."

"Well then we can be good right back to her. Help along her friend-ship with Charley. She could use a friend. Sounds like a nice arrangement for everyone."

"Don't be messing with this. We get on her wrong side, we risk losing everything. Everything, woman! Do you understand that?"

"Sure thing, Frank. Just let nature take its course. What harm is there inviting them on a picnic with us?"

"You're not going to let up till I go over there, are you? Oh never mind."

"America had often been discovered before Columbus, but it had always been hushed up." OSCAR WILDE

7

On the anniversary of Max Dunlap's death, three days before the news broke that Oscar Wilde had been convicted, Mildred and Edra, thirty-three and twenty-nine respectively, reflected. Although Max taught Mildred to be self-reliant in matters concerning the ranch and business, her parents never taught her how to express herself emotionally. All she knew about showing emotions she learned through relating with Edra, none of which prepared her for her grief when her father died, a void she felt she'd never recover from.

"You look so sad, Mildred."

"I don't know I'll ever get over him not being around anymore."

Edra put a hand on Mildred's shoulder. "Do you want to walk out to their gravesites?"

"God, I loved that man. He worked so hard to give us this. I never want to tear down what he built." Mildred looked around the living room of the small dwelling that Max had built himself. She thought beyond its walls to its privacy, backing on a half-mile dirt drive from the main road that was situated on a down slope of a small valley, shielding their home from view. The nearest neighbor was a mile away. The two-bedroom single-story home was surrounded with trees and foliage, and painted white with a high-pitched roof. The south-facing covered porch provided shade during the summer and kept snow out through the winter. Wild lilacs, irises and daffodils planted along it bloomed in the spring.

"I loved him too. Let's go for that walk, Mil." She gently took Mildred's arm and led her out. The women trod their way, silent in memories, until Edra broke the reverie. "I wonder what he must have felt like when he first came to Red River Pass."

"Couldn't have been easy for him. On his own. But then think of all the suffering others went through journeying out west." Mildred's voice cracked.

A chill went down Edra's spine. "Max used to love to tell the story of the Donner party…how this place was founded. How could anyone have predicted that?" She reflected back on Max telling them that when the news of the Donner Party broke, routes were diverted for those traveling west in search of fortunes in gold. An area south on the Sierra Nevada seemed an excellent place to camp, where the loons migrate in the spring to feed on the Lahontan cutthroat trout in a large natural lake offering abundant riparian foliage, and where pronghorn antelope and deer thrive. Max was among those who pitched tents by the lake when word got back to them about the glut of comers and the cutthroat activities of the miners further west. Fate had dealt him a hand and Max knew exactly what he would do with it.

"Of all things to come up now. It's true, he never left a detail out of that god-awful story."

"Oh I'm sorry, Mil. I didn't mean to. My mind just wandered there."

"No, no, it's okay. There's something about recalling all the stories. That one he used to love to tell because it influenced his own life and brought him to Walker Lake. If he hadn't detoured, like the rest of the travelers, out of the fear, he too would have encountered the elements."

"I can't imagine what it must've been like. Those poor people anticipated a shortcut, which ended up taking them three weeks longer than if they'd stayed on the California Trail to begin with. Can you imagine that?"

"That was a bad snowstorm they got trapped in."

Edra smiled, "I can just see Max coming upon the Walker River Valley with such a good range, and falling to the ground."

"Edra, that's why he settled here. He had already heard that the weather was hospitable most year-round. But more importantly he knew, when he saw all the meadow grass, that anyone settling here and owning cattle could fatten them for years. He said it was the smartest move of his life. Then he got lucky."

Edra questioned, "Lucky?"

"He never told you about his filing his Preemption Act claim?"

"I don't recall he did."

Mildred continued, "It provided him a legal and viable means of obtaining land. There was a minimal cost involved to gain title on his original acreage. All he had to do was live on the land for fourteen months and pay a fee. Before long, with the savings he had from doing odd jobs in Ohio, he bought up every available adjacent parcel of land from ranchers who had fallen on hard luck. While other cattle barons had large ranches, they owned only a fraction of the acreage on which their cattle grazed because much of the land was public domain. He told me he felt he was finally making up for his lost and unhappy past growing up in Ohio, where he hated the way his hometown had treated his parents."

"You mean what he told us about his brother Ben and Jessie Buckstorm. He thought all the gossip had something to do with his brother's untimely and mysterious death."

"Yes." Mildred looked off at a few birds flying overhead, and with a saddened tone continued, "I think that's why he didn't like attending church."

"Your mamma struggled with that. I felt guilty that I…"

"Don't Edra. It wasn't your fault. No one faulted you for not wanting to go to town after…"

"Hard not to think I might have had something to do with it."

"It wasn't your fault. Neither was your mother's death."

"If I wasn't born, she'd still be alive." Edra broke down in tears recounting how she had learned about the death of her parents. Four years after Max and Sadie married, Max's first cousin Terrance Fitzgerald with his wife Bettina made the trek from Ohio to Nevada to settle in with the Dunlaps. Bettina, eight months pregnant at the time and weak from journey sickness, arrived dehydrated and in premature labor. Edra was born with so much difficulty that it took Betinna's life. Terrance did not recover from the loss of his wife and shortly thereafter took ill and died from pneumonia. The Dunlaps adopted Edra.

"Hard not to think of all these things now. Let's talk about something a little happier. Max would have wanted that." Mildred took hold of Edra's hand. "Remember how he met mamma?"

Edra smiled and wiped the tears from her cheeks with the sleeve of her dress. "It was when she came with her parents...her father took a position with his cousin Frank Bell supervising the construction of the transcontinental telegraph lines through Nevada."

"Good old Bell money." Mildred squeezed her grip on Edra's hand. "Max knew what he wanted."

"But they loved each other," Edra responded.

"Yes, luckily they did. Mamma was a good woman. But it was pappa who gave us all this." Mildred gestured at the land surrounding them. At Max's death, in 1890 at the age of sixty-four, Mildred had inherited all the wealth that Max acquired in his life, including the ranch and several buildings in Red River Pass as well as ownership of its bank, managed by businessmen in Carson City. After her father died she sold off her cattle, kept the ranch house and surrounding acres for her and Edra, divided up the rest of the land into large parcels, and rented them out to cattle ranchers. Not all the tenants were able to pay cash on a monthly basis, leading her to enter into other contract agreements, which was the case with the Whitmores, just over the hill. Part of their rent was covered through sharecropping and cattle. Mildred received both a portion of the proceeds from the sale of their crops and cattle, and the meat of slaughtered steers. When years were slim pickings she received nothing, forgave missed payments, and authorized the bank in town to loan funds to help families see their way through rough winters. To her credit, she was demure about it.

"I'm grateful for our lives and what he left us, Mil."

"Edra Fitzgerald, that's the first time I ever heard you say 'what he left us' and I'm proud of you."

"You've been saying it to me for years. I always felt it was yours. Not ours. Felt I was lucky enough just to love you and know you'd do right by me."

"Why Edra, you sound like you're accepting that all I have is equally yours. All of this and everything else left to me. None of it would mean anything without you."

They quietly reflected back on memories of Max until Edra broke the silence. "It's hard to believe it's already been five years."

Mildred and Edra walked past the pens where they kept the horses, chickens, pigs, a couple of milk-giving cows, and had a vegetable garden. There, beyond the planted patches of carrots, potatoes, celery, parsnips, and other sprouting vegetables, were Max and Sadie's headstones.

"He loved his garden. No better place for him to rest." A solitary tear drifted down Mildred's cheek.

As Edra looked at Max's headstone, she remembered earlier times of him holding her, playing with her, and chasing her through the house from room to room. She remembered when Max had decided to furnish the back part of the house with a double brass bed, a walnut cabinet for hanging clothes, and a chestnut dresser with a marble top and matching mirror. She found spaces behind the furniture to hide when they played hide and seek. She recalled bruises from banging into the pedal sewing machine in the second bedroom that she had shared with Mildred. She loved Sadie's sterling toilet set and floral china wash pitcher and bowl that sat on the dresser, the pine floors covered with thick wool rugs offering protection from the severest winter cold when the potbellied stoves and woven wool inner curtains seemed inadequate.

With the memory of every little thing in its place, Edra knew that her Uncle Max had toiled for all that he had possessed. "He was a good man. We're lucky we had him for as long as we did," she remarked.

The women stood silent for some time before they headed back to the house. Just outside the front door, off to the west side, was an outhouse. Max never felt he needed to install indoor plumbing because he appreciated keeping the family close to a natural way of living.

"I could have done without that in the winter," Mildred commented with a laugh as they moved past the outhouse to the hitching post outside the front door. From this vantage point they had a view of the barn not far away down a dirt trail. Next to the barn was a building that housed additional hay and feed to sustain livestock through winter months. "And that," Mildred motioned to the barn. "I did not appreciate walking down there when it was cold."

Edra looked at Mildred and smiled. They continued to reminisce, unaware that the next seventy-two hours would bring the news announcing the conviction of Oscar Wilde.

"A woman's face is her work of fiction." OSCAR WILDE

8

Helene arrived home just in time to begin dinner. She had been in town shopping and visiting with Charley. She pulled potatoes from the storage bin, placed them on the cutting board, and began to slice them into tiny pieces. "I'm exhausted," she mumbled.

"What's for eats?" Frank asked as he watched.

"Stew."

"Again? Come home earlier you could get something else on the table for a change!"

"And ignore Charley?" she said with annoyance. "I told you I...we needed help with him. I can't just ignore..." She was playing this to get what she wanted and was determined not to let up if there was any hope of Charley latching onto Mildred. Very little had been on her mind since her earlier conversation with Frank about getting them together.

"Helene, we both know what you're up to."

"Oh yeah, Mildred came by also. Seems she was out shopping by Gus's and wanted to drop something off for Charley."

"Oh?"

"They were pretty friendly."

"Helene!" He smacked his lips in disgust.

"It's supposed to be warm tomorrow. Be a good day for that picnic. How's about after dinner you go over to Mildred's?"

"I'm not going over there that late," he protested.

"You promised…"

"No."

"You haven't been back there since your last visit," she nudged. "She must be wondering why you stopped by."

"I said no!"

"But…you promised," she whined.

"I made no such promise. Now, cut it out, woman."

"Frrrrrrrrrrank," she moaned, "pleeeeeeeeease, just this once. We owe it to her to thank her for helping Charley." She moved closer to him in a manipulative sensual gesture to get what she wanted. It spoke to him that if he did what she wanted he'd get lucky.

"God damn it, Helene! If Mildred was there today just let it be."

"I got food for a picnic. Enough for all of us. It'll spoil…go to waste. Come on, honey." She rubbed his back. "It's just a picnic. What's the harm?"

He felt a rousing in his groin mixed in with all the anger, and he resented that she had that effect on him. He softened and reached back for her.

"Go on over there, honey. I'll get dinner ready then have a wash up and after the kids are down…" Her hand moved down to his thigh.

"Just this once. Do not ask me to do anything like this again."

"Ohhhhhhh, sweetie." Her hand moved higher to latch onto his hardness.

"I'll go in the morning. It's too late now."

"It's not that late." She pulled back.

"Knock it off. I said I'd go in the morning. Don't want to be bothering them if they're eating."

"Go after dinner."

"In the morning."

"You promise? You absolutely swear?" Her voice softened.

"In the morning." He reached for her, pulled her in close, and whispered, "You know what I want for dessert."

"Frank…" she whispered. "When you go…bring Mabel."

*

Nighttime merged into a new day that brought a rooster's crow with the rising sun. Charley awoke to the sound of the cock and the sunshine flooding in through his bedroom window. This was the first morning as far back as he could remember that it felt good to be alive. The change had come slowly, starting with that first visit from Mabel and Mildred. He knew he would never have another love like Emma, but strangely enough, he was taking a liking to Mildred. He was becoming aware that he looked forward to seeing her, talking with her, and that there was something about her that made him feel comfortable. He knew it was not her looks or how she dressed, not the usual attraction. What he felt with Mildred was a kinship. He liked how they related. He liked her lack of pretense and ability to talk about things other people in town did not show an interest in, especially the women who were overly involved in teacup tattle. He never liked that aspect of living in a small town.

*

Frank made his way to the Dunlap's ranch with Mabel in tow. He approached the front door and knocked.

"You here again, Frank? Everything okay?" Mildred asked as she pushed opened the door and came onto the porch. "Hi Mabel." She placed her hand on Mabel's head.

"Everything's fine. Just fine," Frank replied.

Mildred was puzzled. "Then why are you here, Frank?"

"We'd like you to come along with us to the lake today. It's going to be a warm one. Helene packed a basket full of food to feed us all and we'd love to have you."

Mildred was taken aback. She and Edra had never been invited anywhere by the Whitmores. "Why, that's awfully nice of you but I have a lot of chores to do here. You let things go one day and well, you know, Frank, it all just piles up."

"You'd be doing me a big favor if you came along, Mildred." He looked down at Mabel who was fidgeting. "Helene'd be pretty disappointed. Helene was up half the night making chicken, potatoes, bread and gravy, all freshly baked. Mildred, we sure do wish…"

Mabel sprang in, "Uncle Charley's gonna come."

Mildred felt a flush on her face and hoped it didn't show. "Oh, I see." She didn't have time to think of a response and hated to make snap decisions. She needed to plan, anticipate things in advance and then make her moves to avoid doing something she'd regret later. Her hands shook, the moment filled with awkwardness. "Can you give me a minute?"

Before Mildred made her way back in, Edra came out through the door. She had been listening in on their conversation and knew Mildred was in a precarious position with having to make a spur-of-the-moment decision, and how much she hated to do that. Mildred had always been the planner in their relationship, working things out, anticipating con-sequences, and was not spontaneous. Edra felt conflicted. She wanted to help Mildred out and felt guilty she had cast doubt on everything Mildred had worked out to protect them, but she was also scared of where this was all heading. In the end, she decided to stuff her counter feelings and show more support. "Oh, go on. Be good for you to get out."

Mabel tugged on Mildred's dress. "Come on, Mildred."

Mildred felt trapped. "Excuse me a minute please?"

"Hurry up! Let's go!" begged a very impatient Mabel.

Mildred left Frank and Mabel on the porch and took Edra into their bedroom. "Why'd you say that?"

"Don't you want to set up appearances?"

"But I thought you…what am I going to do with the Whitmores being there? I need to think this through and…"

"What's there to think? No way you're going to predict what's going to happen, so might as well seize the opportunity to make a show of attention to Charley."

Mildred was amazed with Edra's change of attitude. "Whatever…"

Edra looked deep into Mildred's eyes. They knew each other well and in this moment, like so many that came before, they honed in on what they felt and were thinking without words needing to pass between them. It was times like this, in their hearts' synchronicity, that they knew the only answer was to continue to love, despite everything. Edra watched as the fear drained from Mildred's face. It was the validation that she needed that by following her intuitive sense she was doing the right thing. When their silence broke, Edra spoke. "It's okay." And she meant it in that moment where the feelings of insecurity took a rest and the hope that Mildred had been right about things working out was true. "Besides, it might be better for you to be with Charley along with a group than alone with him."

Mildred agreed, got ready and went along with Frank and Mabel. They circled by the Whitmore's to pick up Helene and little Frankie, and then headed to town to rustle up Charley.

On the ride out to the lake, Charley made small conversation with Mildred as they sat together in the back of the carriage. "That lake has some interesting history."

"Yes, so I've been told," replied Mildred, who had not only heard the stories of Walker Lake from her father, but had done extensive reading on the subject.

"Did you know that Joseph Reddeford Walker of Tennessee led a fur-trapping expedition into this area? The first battle between the whites and Indians was in this territory."

"Oh that's interesting." Mildred politely kept quiet about the fact that she knew the story. She also knew that to be a good listener helped to make people feel better about themselves.

"Did you hear about the time he was traveling from north to south exploring the Humboldt River more thoroughly, and that is how he discovered our lake?"

"Sounds interesting, Charley."

"As Walker approached with his men, a large group of Indians suddenly appeared from their hiding places in the tall grass. Walker's men pointed their guns at the Indians to exhibit their weapons but the Indians had never seen guns before," Charley laughed.

Mildred, trying to contain her boredom, smiled back.

"The Indians wanted to see what effect the guns would have on some ducks swimming near the shore of the lake. When the men fired, the Indians fell to the ground, more astonished by the noise than the fact that the firings killed several ducks," Charley continued.

Helene turned around and glanced at Charley and Mildred. She gave Frank a gentle elbow to his ribs and whispered, "See...they're getting on well."

Frank shot her a look.

"Several months later, Walker led a large-scale battle, defeating the Indians. Walker Lake was named after this victory," Charley droned.

Mildred listened as Charley rambled on about how tribes of Indians were pacified when emissaries sent by the Federal Government managed to persuade them to give up their wandering way of life and settle on reservations. "People come to Walker Lake for lots of reasons," he continued, "the history...the breathtaking scenery."

Mildred was familiar with the one-hundred-square-mile expanse nestled at the base of Mount Grant. The hovering snow-covered peak and hills made a spectacular backdrop for the mostly unfruitful shoreline, punctuated here and there by groves of trees or bushes and rushes sprouting from the water. The deep blue color of the lake contrasted with the surrounding hills, covered with brown grass and sagebrush that turned red in the setting sun. The river, feeding the lake, provided not only a visual delight, but was a ribbon of life in the otherwise barren landscape, providing water and grass for horses and cattle, and shade from the bushes and trees along its banks. She sympathized with how the Indians must have felt, being manipulated out of their way of life and forced into a form of slavery on reservations. She felt a thread of entrapment running through her with having to contend with Charley's rambling and going along with her plan in the first place. She resented why she felt she had to put herself in that position and forced herself to make conversation. "What an interesting story, Charley. You sure do know your history. Do you read a lot?"

"No, not much. I learned that from helping the children at school. I was volunteering there before Emma took ill." Charley became quiet.

At a loss for words, Mildred sat still for a while and then broke the silence. "Do you ever fish, Charley?"

"Matter of fact I've been out here and caught some trout. Cooked them right here at the lake."

Mildred knew the lake was famous for its Lahontan cutthroat trout, and just as she was contemplating a time when Max had brought a load of them home, a flock of migrating loons flew by. "I guess it's the fish that bring all these birds to the area," she commented.

Charley looked to the sky as the flock circled down toward the water. "You bet. This here lake is an excellent feeding ground for all sorts of birds."

Frank pulled up the carriage and settled the horses in the shade next to several other buggies and carriages of families that had arrived before them. The group made their way to a cluster of cottonwood and poplar trees surrounded by tall grass. It was a perfect place to stay comfortable away from the heat.

Mildred helped Helene unpack the lunch onto the blanket.

"That sure is a calm lake today," Frank commented as he bit into a chicken leg.

Mildred watched the ripples cast by the swimmers splashing about that shimmered on the glassy surface of the water. The sun was fixed in the cloudless sky, baking everything in its rays. There was an uncharacteristic lack of wind, not even the slightest breeze on this sultry July day. It was not unlike the day of Edra's twelfth birthday. Mildred smiled as she remembered that day, spooned some potato salad into her mouth, then replied. "Yes, it's very still, Frank."

"That was just about the tastiest chicken you ever made, Helene," said Charley as he wiped his lips with a napkin. "Boy, it's a warm one today."

"I'm hot, mamma. Let's go to the water," Mabel urged as she jumped up and started to run to the carriage to get her swimsuit.

"Mabel, you calm down. Let your food settle," Helene said.

"Mamma!"

"Hush now, young lady." Helene began to clean up leftover food and put it back into her basket.

"I'm stuffed," said Frank. "How's about a smoke, Charley?"

"Frank, I think I'll pass on that right now. I feel like getting up and stretching. Anyone for a little walk?"

"It's too hot," said Helene. "We'll just settle here a bit then take the kids in the water."

"Let's go now!" Mabel nudged her mother.

"Mabel Whitmore, you sit yourself down till your mamma gets this blanket cleared. You heard what she said to you." Frank's voice was stern.

As Mabel began to pout, Mildred decided that she'd had about all she could take. "Sure, Charley," she said as she stood up to join him.

✳

Joshua and Annalee Smartley with their three children had also decided that this would be a perfect day to escape the heat and relax at Walker Lake.

"I tell you there isn't going to be any letting up on this for a while. It's just simply repulsive," Annalee said, referring to the latest development that had come down the telegraph pipeline about Oscar Wilde. It was no mystery that the press kept fueling his imprisonment. News of Wilde sold papers and provided relief from the ennui many experienced, which included Annalee. He was the perfect antidote for her dull life. "He's eating watery porridge and bread."

Joshua replied, "He's lucky they aren't starving him to death."

"I'm glad he's not getting any books, paper or pens. Let him sit on his wooden bed and be reminded that his kind of behavior won't be tolerated. If he thought he was going to have an easy time of prison, he's got another thing…"

"Look who's coming our way," Joshua piped in. "Well I'll be…"

"Who?" Annalee craned her neck to see who he meant, but the two people approaching were outside her peripheral vision. "Who?" she repeated.

"It's Charley with Mildred."

Annalee, without thinking, abruptly stood and turned to face them. "Charley! Charley Milpass!"

A pang of adrenaline shot through Mildred. It was fortuitous to run into one of Josie's cohorts, but she was unprepared for the anxiety she felt. It was new and frightening for her to feel so out of control. There was no running away, no jumping on her horse and avoiding what was coming, no moving on past the crowd of jeers and making fun of her. She was trapped. She smiled in an attempt to cover up how she felt and moved a hand over her forehead, stroking her hair back, in a discrete attempt to wipe away beads of sweat.

Annalee reached them, slightly short of breath.

"Hello, Annalee. How are you folks doing today?" Charley could have cared less about having any conversation with them but determined the easiest way out would be civility.

"So you're out and about? I heard you were doing better. Josie told me you come out of your funk." Annalee looked straight at Charley, completely ignoring Mildred.

Mildred stood there listening to the noises coming out of their mouths and tried to maintain composure. She imagined what Annalee must be thinking and felt anger rise within her from all the years of persecution she had endured. She would have liked to slap Annalee across the face to shut her up. She wanted to get the hell away from the chattering. When they finally moved along, it was all Mildred could do to keep from vomiting her lunch.

"Most people are other people. Their thoughts are someone else's opinions, their lives a mimicry, their passions a quotation." OSCAR WILDE

9

Annalee woke up at the crack of dawn, threw on a robe, grabbed a basket and made her way to the chicken coop to fetch some eggs. She was beside herself in anticipation of her visit to Sarah Funkle. The gossip over Oscar Wilde had given her and her friends plenty to chatter over at teatime, and now she was about to add new excitement.

Annalee stood nervously at the Funkle's front door. As Sarah opened the door, Annalee greeted her with, "Glorious day. Brought you some eggs here. Enough for you and Pursey. The rest I'll give to Josie and Satchel."

"Mighty nice of you coming out here so early. We'll be sure to use these fresh eggs today."

Annalee stood nearly bursting with impatience as she waited for Sarah to invite her in.

Sarah saw that Annalee had something on her mind. "Would you like to come in and have a cup of coffee?"

"Why, I thought you'd never ask." Annalee barged through the door. "You are not going to believe who I saw yesterday at the lake!"

"Why, who?" Sarah led the way to the kitchen to prepare the coffee.

THE PERSECUTION OF MILDRED DUNLAP

Annalee had a difficult time holding back her words. She wanted them to come out slow and easy, not unlike how she had trained herself when having sex with Joshua, in order to savor the experience and build on every moment to the juicy expectation she hoped for. She felt the prickly pins running down her spine, the anticipation sensually exhilarating, and she didn't want to spoil it by rushing through like Joshua did when he had gone without for a fortnight. "Charley and Mildred! They were holding hands," Annalee lied. "Why, that woman has to be the ugliest thing I've ever seen. How could Charley…"

Sarah could not believe her ears. "You mean they were together there? Alone? Surely you're kidding."

"This is no joke. That homely woman has got her clutches into Charley and only heaven knows why he seems to be enjoying it," replied Annalee.

"Why, that ugly spinster. He's got to be after her money. There's no way in the world…"

"Oh I could not agree more. There's something on his mind and it's got nothing to do with liking that woman."

"Emma would turn in her grave. Mildred Dunlap!"

Sarah threw Annalee a look of mischief. "I'm going with you to Josie's!"

Annalee's story threw Josie Purdue into a dither. "No one in their right mind would be a friend with the likes of Mildred. But Charley? It doesn't figure. I bet he's wanting to be with someone, you know…who he don't have to feel nothing for. He can have what he will with her. All that money. He'll not worry about anything ever again." She shook her head in disgust. "But with that woman? Not enough money in the whole world… I can't stand the sight of her!" Josie's resentment was nothing new, but since Mildred was the brunt of ridicule and jokes in town, no one ever questioned her about it.

"But he loved Emma," Annalee replied.

"He went through a year of hell with Emma taking ill. He's probably relieved he don't have to change her diapers no more. Good riddance!" Josie slapped her hands together to make her point.

"Josie!" Sarah exclaimed. "He loved Emma."

"Love? What do any of us know about what goes on in someone's home? Why that wife of his and all her pain brought the whole town down there to cater to Charley. People ought to just die and let us move on with our lives."

"Josie! What's gotten into you?" Annalee admonished.

A nerve had been struck with the first mention of Mildred and Josie was not to concede that it bothered her. The boiling inside was exploding. "Me? Look who's talking. We're all sitting here enjoying this. Am I saying anything someone isn't thinking?"

"Well yes, but…"

"So, I'm saying it. Let me talk! That Charley and Mildred are up to no good."

Eventually, the blabfest petered out as the women became exhausted with Josie's tirade and repeating themselves, signaling that it was time to leave. On their way out, Annalee and Sarah ran into Madeline Trentwood.

*

Madeline made her way to Gus Spivey's General Store. She entered to find Gus stocking the shelves with supplies that had just arrived. "And how are you doing, Gus?" She was in a perky mood.

"I'm well, Madeline. I'll be just a couple minutes here then I'll be with you."

Madeline glanced around to see who else was in the store and when she saw Rebecca Jenkins, she thought twice about going over to her. Rebecca, the minister's wife, would not take kindly to an earful of gossip about Charley, especially since the recent passing of his wife. Rebecca was a decent woman who helped her husband Amos with church events that included anything from tending to the children on Sunday to helping arrange weddings and funerals. Instead, Madeline paced about and fiddled with the goods on the shelves.

When Gus finished stocking the last shelf with tea, he asked Madeline, "What can I do for you?"

She smiled, but appeared anxious. "I'll be needing some flour,

64

sugar, and let's see..." She hesitated then pulled a list from her pocket. "Do you have cloverine salve?"

"Yes, we have that." He reached for the tin of salve from the shelf behind him then turned back toward her. "How much flour do you want today?"

She pointed to the bag she wanted. "That should do me. I'm going to make a nice big cake. The girls are having a tea tomorrow and I want to bring something special. Would you like me to come by and bring you a piece?"

"Well, you are in a good mood today." Gus smiled.

"You just never know..." She grinned like the Cheshire cat. "We have more to catch up on," she blurted incomprehensibly.

"We?" he asked.

"Me, Josie, Sarah, and Annalee."

"Oh I see." He instantly knew to avoid asking her anything further.

That did not deter Madeline. "Annalee was out and about with eggs. And stories."

Gus readied the flour and the rest of the items on Madeline's list. "That'll be..."

Madeline noticed Rebecca was out of earshot and interrupted, "You'll never guess who's going out with Charley Milpass! If Annalee hadn't seen them with her own eyes, I'd never believe it. But I tell you Gus, it's true as the moon rises in the sky."

"That'll be fifty-seven cents."

"Mildred! That's who. Can you believe it? Charley was out at the lake with her."

Gus began to feel cornered as Madeline continued to replay the scuttlebutt until Rebecca approached the counter to pay her bill. To Gus's relief, Madeline became quiet.

A few more customers walked into the store, one of them Charley. When Madeline saw Charley, her face flushed, she paid her bill, and left. Gus was amused as he watched her walk out.

"Hey there, Gus. How's it going today?" Charley asked innocently.

"Just been taking in an earful," Gus blurted without thinking.

"Seems the town's in an uproar over you and Mildred."

"What on earth are you talking about?" Charley asked.

"Your date with Mildred."

It took Charley a moment to tie the pieces together, and then it dawned on him. "Who have you been talking to? I knew Annalee couldn't keep that dang mouth of hers shut. I knew it the minute I saw her. Can't somebody have a friend without people butting in and making trouble? What is the matter with those people?"

Seeing that he'd hit a nerve, Gus tried to back-pedal and undo the slip. "They just want to see you happy, Charley."

"That's nonsense Gus, and you know it."

"There's a lot of people care about you here. Look how many rallied to help you out…" Gus did not finish his thought. He didn't want to bring up Emma and hit another nerve.

"You think so?" Charley oozed sarcasm. "Not one of them bothered to talk to me except Mildred. Everyone just rushing in and out pushing food at me not knowing what to say so they end up saying damn stupid things. Mildred comes along and she's genuinely nice. People been judging her wrong."

"No offense, but her looks… I know she can't help it. People like to talk. All the things been said through the years."

"Well, don't you be adding to it! Not you too, Gus! Don't be saying anything when you don't know a thing about her. What do you know about someone who's helped me when I didn't want no more of this world? She's a good woman. I don't take too kindly to what you just implied!" Charley surprised himself in his defense of Mildred. He knew the talk: *She's plain looking, overly endowed and unattractive, too full in figure, unaware of her appearance.* She was nothing in comparison to Emma, who was a raving beauty, yet he was drawn to Mildred. In her, he saw something he liked, an inner glow and aliveness that made him feel good to be around. As time progressed and he got to know her better, he stopped caring about what she looked like, what others were saying, and more about what he saw in her. To him she was real and he valued that in his new friend.

"Whoa Charley, I don't mean no harm."

"Don't be thinking of saying anything about her to me that's not nice!" Charley held up his fist to Gus's face.

"Hey. Hey there now. I didn't mean anything. I was just repeating what I had heard. I didn't think it would bother you this much."

"Well now you know different." Charley was fuming.

"Okay, Charley. You sure are hot under the collar. Calm down. If you're happy, then old Gus is happy. How's about a little drink?" Gus went to the end of the counter, bent down, and brought up a bottle of whiskey and two shot glasses. He filled the glasses and handed one to Charley. "Here you go. Let what was said be bygones. I didn't mean any harm."

Charley grabbed the glass, brought it to his lips, and threw it down with a hard swallow. "Okay Gus. You remember what I said. I'm not kidding here."

"Sure thing, Charley." Gus took a swallow from his glass. "Another?"

"No, that's enough for me."

"Well, what can I do for you?" asked Gus.

"That tin of biscuits over there." He pointed to a row of fancy tins on a nearby shelf. "How much?"

"Don't pay me nothing. You take it with my apologies to smooth the words we had between us."

Charley hesitated. With a slight frown he took the tin, gave a nod to Gus and left the store.

By noon the entire town had heard about Charley and Mildred.

"When the gods wish to punish us, they answer our prayers." Oscar Wilde

10

It was a day like any other for Ben Thorndike. He awoke, had breakfast with Rose and the kids, then made his way to Spivey's General Store to pick up supplies. The project on the barn at the Dunlap's ranch was underway and he was glad he'd gotten an early start before winter set in, which would make outside construction impossible.

Gus was talking with a group of women but when he saw Ben he moved away and went to greet him.

"You've got an early crowd here, Gus."

"Ben, I got some new things in I want to show you." Gus gently moved him to the back of the store out of earshot from the others and pretended to be pointing out some merchandise.

"You heading out to Mildred's now?" Gus asked.

"After I get a few things here. Why?"

"The town's in an uproar that shows no sign of quitting any time soon. It's a little out of control. I mentioned it to Charley, which upset him."

Ben looked confused. "What are you talking about?"

Gus relayed what he had heard from Madeline. "Now these ladies are here getting fixings to have a baking party today and you can guess what they're going to be cooking up inside those busy little heads of theirs. Thought you ought to know. Never been anything like this involving Mildred before."

Ben nodded. "Oh man."

After he purchased what he needed, Ben made his way out to Mildred's, not sure what to do. Although he felt protective of Mildred, he had never gotten into her affairs before, but this was different. He did not want to see her ambushed when she went into town, and he definitely did not want turmoil coming back to Edra either with all that she had already lived through. He decided he needed to say something and that would best be coming from him. He made his way to the front door and knocked.

"Morning, Ben," greeted Edra as she swung open the door.

"Morning, Edra. Is Mildred in?"

"Why yes, let me get her."

Edra called to Mildred that Ben was there to see her, and then returned to the kitchen to finish cleaning up from breakfast. She made a point to stay within listening range.

"Morning, Ben. How's the barn coming along?"

"Just fine, Mildred. No problems." He paused. "Not there at least."

"Is there something else wrong?" Mildred asked curiously.

Ben felt his nerves getting the better of him. His hands were sweating and he felt a tight constriction in his throat. "Mildred," he sighed, "I don't like to be into your business, but I heard something disturbing in town and wanted you to hear it from a friend."

Mildred stepped back. "Come on in, Ben. Would you like a cup of tea?"

He walked through the door past Mildred and nodded at Edra, who had reentered the dining room.

"Some tea?" Mildred repeated as Ben sat on the couch.

"No, no thank you."

Mildred perched on a chair across from him. "What's on your mind, Ben?"

He shook his head indicating how difficult this was for him. His eyes widened. "I'm going to just come out with it. Gus told me the women in town are in an uproar over you out at the lake with Charley. Some nasty things being said. I really don't want to repeat all of it, but if you…"

"You don't need to repeat anymore. Thank you, Ben. I appreciate your loyalty."

"Sure thing, Mildred. Sorry I had to bring this to you. Well, I'll be getting back to work now."

He stood. So did Mildred. "You did right," she said as she walked him to the door. She gazed after him thoughtfully as he walked off toward the barn.

The conversation hit Edra with a jolt. *Nasty things? What were they? Oh God.* Acid poured into her stomach as adrenaline rushed through her body. The little bit of relief she had felt over supporting Mildred's visit with the Whitmores, out at the lake, vanished like a carcass plucked away by vultures with each word Ben uttered. It wasn't so much the bad news about Mildred that worried her, she'd heard that before, but rather the tone in Ben's voice that gave her a fright. He was not an alarmist, yet he spoke with a concealed agitation belying the calm he was trying to project. It was the undeniable energy in his words that struck Edra and cast a pall over what they were doing.

Mildred saw the color leave Edra's face. "You okay?"

"I just need to be alone for a bit," Edra mumbled as she moved to the bedroom.

Mildred followed her and watched as she reclined on the only bed in the room, the only one in the entire house. The other bedroom had been converted to an office that Mildred used to take care of ranch business. No one had ever entered those two back rooms that they had converted after Mildred's parents died.

What would people think if they saw this? Was it a mistake to get rid of the bed in the spare room? Since the Wilde telegraph, new thoughts like this added to Edra's worry. Broaching the topic with Mildred was met with resistance, so after the third or forth attempt she gave up saying anything, causing her insides to fester.

Mildred sat on the bed next to Edra and gently stroked her forehead. "We knew this could happen. It's what we want. Let them talk all they want about Charley and me. That's the whole point."

"We don't know all they're saying," Edra cried. "Mil, I hate this…"

"Let it out, honey."

Anger mingled with sorrow, Edra pulled back from Mildred's touch. "I don't want to! Why'd we have to disrupt our lives with this stupid plan? Leave me alone."

"I'm not leaving you alone."

Edra screamed, "I'm so mad! Why can't people just leave us alone? What'd we ever do to anyone!" She broke down in tears.

Mildred felt Edra's pain. It was also her pain. Her anger. Her grief. Her frustration. To say anything about how she felt was to risk aggravating Edra more, so she did what she always did, she continued to suppress her own feelings to be strong. She also knew that it was futile to get Edra to see reason, that Charley would never show an interest and the plan would work, a fact she was sure was already happening. She had to let Edra's emotions run their course, which she did as she sat there watching her sob until she fell into an exhausted sleep, then quietly left the bedroom.

*

While Edra was sleeping, Charley had arrived unexpectedly to find Mildred on the front porch reading a book.

Startled, she rose from her chair. "Charley."

He handed her the tin of biscuits. "Brought you these."

Neurons fired at rapid pace, heat flushed through her veins, pupils widened, and her heart sped up as she tried to think what to do. Once again, caught off guard without sufficient time to think was unnerving. She couldn't have Edra wake up to find Charley there and didn't know how to turn him down. *What the hell are you doing here anyway? You can't be coming out here uninvited!* All she could think to say was, "Edra's not feeling well. We better keep our voices down."

"I was hoping we could catch a bite to eat. I guess it's not a good time."

"No, it really isn't…" She caught herself. She had an idea, which might just be the opportunity she needed to calm things and stop the uninvited visits. "On second thought, if we go now, it should be okay. I can't leave her for too long."

"That'd be fine, Mildred. Only if you're sure."

"Just give me a minute to get my hat." She left him on the porch and went inside to leave Edra a note. *Went out with Charley. I'm going to take care of everything. Be back soon. Trust me. Mil.*

When Edra woke, it was to an empty house. In the living room next to a fancy tin of biscuits was a note addressed to her. As she began reading, Ben's buckboard leaving the property distracted her from seeing the whole message. "You went out with him! Oh my God! After what I just went through…" She crumpled the note and threw it to the floor. "You left me…to be with him!" She exploded, stomped around aimlessly, stormed into the kitchen, grabbed a butcher knife near the sink, and smashed it into the cutting board, screaming, "God damn you, Charley!" The next hit of the knife slipped on the wet board and jabbed her other palm, causing a deep gash. "Good!" she screamed. "Bleed! Go on and bleed!"

She threw the knife into the sink with such force that it bounced back in the air, barely missing her and landing on the floor. The path of the knife caused her to jerk back and come to her senses. She grabbed a towel and wrapped her palm tightly as she helplessly sank to the floor in a crying heap.

"America is the only country that went from barbarism to decadence without civilization in between." OSCAR WILDE

11

On the ride into town, Mildred felt disturbed over Edra's reaction. She was glad for the time it took to regain her composure. The slightest display of emotion on her part would undoubtedly be misconstrued and twisted into something against her. She didn't want to fuel the hatred anymore than she absolutely had to, and knew that what was important was to keep the focus on what she needed to accomplish with Charley.

"I thought we'd grab a bite at Barney's. They have some mighty good meat loaf and mashed potatoes."

"That sounds just fine, Charley." Her gut was in knots; the last thing she felt like doing was eating.

"Went there two nights ago and had me some of Pat's great apple pie," Charley droned. "Clotted cream and all. But hey, Mildred, you could have some of Pat's chocolate cake."

"Yes, that would be nice." *Will you stop talking about food!*

As they drove down the main street past the stagecoach office, bank, blacksmith, and on to Barney Green's Hotel and Café, she saw several people stop and take notice of them. She thought she overhead Jake Cummings squeal, *Well, I'll be damned.* A dry heat in the air brought an uncomfortable moisture to her underarms that she hoped wouldn't show. She squirmed to readjust her position on the hard seat and felt relieved when Charley parked the buggy. He got out, walked around to Mildred's side, and helped her down. He looked through the window and noticed Pat Green serving customers. "Pat's here today. I'm sure that means apple pie!"

As Charley held open the door, Mildred nodded and stepped in. A hush fell over the room followed by a few whispers from a table in the back where Sam and Hanah Larue were seated. Mildred averted her eyes, glancing downward. Charley motioned to an empty table in a private corner near the front. "How's that over there?"

"That'd be fine," Mildred replied in a near whisper, following Charley as he made his way to the table. She was glad the room was overly large to allow ample space between the tables. Last thing she wanted was someone close enough to breathe down her back. It was bad enough necks were craned and ears focused on them, even if eyes avoided them. Nothing more than whispers continued for several minutes, broken by Pat's laughter coming from the kitchen, which heightened Mildred's discomfort. The sound of a wooden chair sliding on the worn floor of lumber, followed by another, then footsteps moving in their direction behind Charley sent a surge of intense warmth to Mildred's belly, until they moved on past and out through the door. The couple must have been waiting, after paying their bill, to take in the sight of the new pair in town, the joke of the town. *What's taking Pat so long?* Mildred wanted to eat and leave, and get back to Edra who was preoccupying her mind.

"Yes, they do have meat loaf." He watched her read the daily menu. "What'll ya have?"

"I'm not all that hungry. We had a late breakfast. Let's see."

Charley interrupted Mildred's thought. "How about a sandwich then? Eat what you like and wrap the rest to take back?"

Just as Mildred looked again at the menu, Pat Green approached the table. "Charley, have you decided what you're having?"

"Mildred?" Charley asked, deferring to her.

"What kind of sandwiches do you have?"

"The usual," Pat replied shaking her head, indicating that she thought Mildred's question was stupid.

Charley piped up, "The usual is chicken, ham, and roast beef."

Mildred felt resentment for Pat's rudeness, like Satchel earlier at the telegraph office when he showed her so little attention, and Annabel at the lake who refused to acknowledge her. It was one thing for Annabel to ignore her but to her it was unthinkable to embarrass a customer. She was disgusted that she had to take the abuse and could not just get up and walk out. She was aware they were drawing attention from the other customers. Her only comfort was the idea that Charley felt the same as these people and sooner or later would want to stop seeing her. What she couldn't fathom was why he wanted to spend time with her now when he could have any available woman in town at his side. *He's just not ready but when he is, my plan will be complete. Maybe he's after my money? I don't care what his motive is…just get it over with!* She sucked in a breath of air then spoke calmly to Pat. "I'll have a chicken sand-wich. Thank you."

Pat made a note of the order without looking at Mildred. "Meat loaf for you, Charley? Made it myself this morning."

"Yes."

Pat jotted down Charley's order and headed back to the kitchen, laughing.

Charley looked at Mildred with concern, an expression that he understood Mildred might have been upset with Pat's treatment of her. "You okay?"

"Yes."

"She was lacking her manners with you," Charley said with sympathy. "I never like that sort of thing. I'm sorry for ya, Mildred."

Although she ignored his comment, she noted what seemed a genuine tone of sympathy, which confused her.

Charley continued. "I can understand you not wanting to say nothing in here."

Mildred looked at Charley and shook her head. "It's okay, Charley."

She lowered her voice. "I don't have to live with people who aren't fond of me."

He nodded approval at her reply. He knew her plain looks fed town talk and that she didn't have friends because of it. He remembered what Gus had said. Charley knew what she looked like, her face overly full with a thinning hairline, wrinkles around her eyes and the ridge of her mouth from working out in the sun, and some mannerisms that he felt were a bit too manly, but he didn't care. He didn't care that she wore dark clothes that covered her from neck to ankle and were not flattering for a woman's figure. What he saw in her, what he felt with her, was not a physical attraction, like the passion with Emma; rather something else drew him to her. It was something alive and fresh and spoke to him in a new way and he liked it, a lot. It bothered him what people said about her, how they treated her without giving her a chance.

He was glad when Pat finally approached with their order and wondered if she kept them waiting on purpose. "Man, that looks good." Pat placed the dishes on the table and then left without saying a word. "And smell that gravy," Charley added, making an attempt to lighten up the situation.

They ate in silence as people came and left, icy stares adding to Mildred's discomfort.

Pat approached the table. "Dessert? Apple pie for you, Charley?"

Charley gave Pat a solemn look. "Nothing else. This should cover it," he said as he handed her payment for the meal.

Pat smiled at Charley. "Ya'll come back now."

Charley helped Mildred out of her seat. They left and climbed back into the buggy. On the way to Mildred's place, close to thirty minutes had gone by in silence until Mildred said, "Thank you for taking me out, Charley."

He replied. "Wish it were more pleasant for you. I don't know how you put up with all that nonsense."

"Had it all my life. You get used to it."

He shook his head and was at a loss for what to say.

Once again, what seemed like empathy on his part confused her.

It was an unintended action that presented a doubt on how her plan would turn out, which she quickly dismissed as ridiculous. In a soft voice, she said, "I need to tell you something, Charley, and sure do hope you understand."

"Sure, Mildred."

"Edra's had a rough life. I think just about everyone in town knows what she's been through."

Charley nodded. He noticed an inflection in her voice when she mentioned Edra's name, a softness.

"I try to keep a watch on her. I don't think it's a good idea for any-one to come out to the ranch unannounced. It might scare her."

Charley replied in a concerned tone, "I completely forgot about that when I came around, Mildred. I just wanted to pay my respects and thank you for being kind to me. I won't come around anymore."

Charley's explanation for why he showed up at the ranch eased some of her tension. *So it was just a friendly visit to thank me.* With a return of emotional composure, she raised her voice a little. "No, I didn't mean that. I just need to know beforehand. Ben comes and goes. If you could send a note with him."

"You sure that's okay with you?"

"Sure thing, Charley. I just need you to understand Edra needs me to help her. She doesn't really trust anyone else since…you understand, don't you?" Mildred said, with the intent to pave the way for future excuses to keep the boundaries with Charley under her control, to keep a balance between showing interest in him and maintaining her life with Edra.

Charley smiled at Mildred to let her know that he understood. They rode the rest of the way without saying another word. Back at Mildred's front door he said, "I'll get that note out to you."

*

The first thing Mildred noticed when entering the house was the mess in the living room. The note she had written had been crumpled and thrown onto the floor. A vase lay shattered beside it, and fruit from the bowl on the dining room table was scattered all over the place.

When she saw the blood on the kitchen counter she panicked and ran to the bedroom where she found Edra huddled on the bed, dark circles under her bloodshot eyes, with her hand wrapped in a bloodsoaked cloth. "What…"

"It was an accident."

"That whole mess was an accident?"

"Yes." She turned her back to Mildred.

"What the hell's going on here?" She moved around the bed to face Edra.

"Leave me alone."

"I'm not going anywhere till you tell me what's going on. Stop acting like a baby and talk to me."

"A baby! Leave me alone! Get out! That's what you want anyway!"

"Stop this, right now." She sat down on the bed and grabbed hold of Edra and pulled her close. "You're scaring me. Talk to me."

Mildred held her so tightly it broke Edra's resistance and with that came another river of tears. "You left…"

"Go on. I'm here now."

"You went with him."

"He came out here. He just showed up. I went with him so that wouldn't happen again. I went to take care of that. I wrote that in the note."

"No, you didn't."

Mildred released her grip and got the note. "Look here…"

Edra could barely see the words on the page but at the bottom was the part she hadn't read. "I didn't see that." She wiped a tear from her cheek and spoke in a whisper. "I told you he likes you…he came all the way out here. When I woke up and you were gone…after what happened…you left me, to be with him. Why'd you do that?"

"Maybe it wasn't such a good idea. I thought if I went with him we'd be seen together…I told him he can't come out unannounced anymore. I shouldn't have gone. You know I'm not good with spontaneous decisions. I told him I didn't want to leave you."

"So why did you?"

78

"I had a second thought. Kill two birds...never mind all that. It was a bad idea. I'm really sorry."

"Mil, I don't know what I'd ever do without you."

"I feel the same, honey. It's not going to happen." She looked down at Edra's hand. "How'd that happen?"

Edra told her.

"Morality, like art, means drawing a line someplace." OSCAR WILDE

12

Mildred ran through the door screaming, They're coming! They found out! Run Edra, run! Her dress caught on the door, paralyzing her motion. There was nothing she could do now but watch them approach with lit torches.

She heard a distant voice calling to her. It was hard to make out what it was saying. She tried to focus her attention on the voice. She felt a rolling motion move her body. It was making her feel sick. Stop! I did nothing wrong! Don't hurt me. Run Edra!

"Run, Edra!" Mildred screamed.

"Mil." Edra cried as she continued to shake Mildred's shoulder trying to wake her up.

Mildred tossed around on the bed, sweat pouring from her body. In a dazed state she heard Edra's voice.

"What?" She opened her eyes and felt an instant sense of relief. "That was some dream."

"More like a nightmare."

"It was so real."

Edra wiped the dripping sweat from Mildred's forehead and pulled the sheet down from around her neck. "You're soaking wet. You were moaning and calling out my name."

It had been a week since Mildred's date with Charley. He had sent a note out with Ben but she had replied that she would have to get back to him, that Edra was ill and she had her hands full. She hated lying but didn't know what else to do to stall him to allow for things to cool off.

"Come on Mildred, you need to get out of that wet nightie. That's the third bad dream this week." Edra stood from where she was sitting at the side of the bed. She unbuttoned her nightgown, shook her arms from the sleeves, and let it fall to the ground. "Wash day today. Let's get those sheets off."

Mildred observed Edra's silhouette, full breasts, flat abdomen, tiny waist, curved hips, long slender legs, and milky complexion. The sun shone through strands of hair that had fallen from their tie, cascading down her neck and smooth back. "You are so beautiful."

Edra smiled. "Up!" She put out a hand to Mildred.

Mildred pulled her back down next to her. "I love you. I don't ever want you to doubt that again." She caressed the back of Edra's neck and pulled her face next to hers. "I would die for you." Their lips met and for the first time in three weeks they made love.

An hour later as they lay with their arms around each other, Edra whispered, "I needed that."

Mildred gently stroked Edra's abdomen. "It's been too long."

The moment was instantly lost when the women got out of bed and Edra noticed blood on the backside of Mildred's nightgown. "There's blood…" She saw more on her hand. She knew it was only a few days since Mildred had finished her last overly heavy period. "This hasn't happened before." She watched Mildred use the nightie she was wearing to catch the moisture from between her legs as she went to get a pad.

"Just my monthly." Mildred disliked making her own pads out of sponge material wrapped in soft cotton but refused to order them through Gus's catalogues. She wanted no part in using a mail order product for something that personal.

"You just had your period."

"It's just coming again early."

"Early? You had it a few days ago…this isn't right." Edra was worried that her emotional overreacting was the problem. Her pattern, to take things personally, started when her parents died. When it would come up through the years, Max tried to tell her it wasn't her fault, to no avail. Even after the rape, she wondered what she had done wrong to deserve it. This deep overly sensitive flaw found no solace in Mildred's attempts to get her to see reason, things in logical fashion as they actually occurred and not how she thought they happened. As her relationship with Mildred developed and trust grew, she learned to cope through the security it brought, but she knew that if anything were to happen to Mildred it would threaten her very existence. "I'm sorry."

"Oh Edra, honey. You've done nothing to apologize for…"

"Yes I did. My outburst."

"I think that was a good thing. Got it out of your system."

"Yeah, and put it into yours."

"Boy, I wish I had that much power on someone else." Mildred laughed in an attempt to lighten things up. This usually worked.

"It's not funny this time. I mean it," Edra pouted.

Mildred knew they'd hit an impasse and when that happened nothing short of distraction worked, which usually broke the cycle. "Oh come on, honey. We both know that my monthly comes early at times. You're making way too much of this. Let me get cleaned up. How about making some coffee?"

Edra threw on a robe and went to the kitchen to prepare coffee and breakfast while Mildred cleaned up.

"That smells good." Mildred picked up the cup.

The guilt Edra felt had receded. "I added a little cinnamon."

Mildred, relieved the mood had passed, smiled. "Hey, that's a great idea."

"So, when are you going to see Charley again?"

Mildred hesitated, took a sip of coffee, and looked at Edra doubt-fully. "You sure?"

"As sure as I'm gonna be."

"Okay then, I'll send a note with Ben and have him come around tomorrow." Mildred hesitated. "Or is that too soon?"

"That's fine."

Mildred took another sip of coffee. "I think it's smart that we don't keep putting him off. Oh!" Mildred grabbed her stomach.

It startled Edra. "What…"

Mildred abruptly pushed her chair back from the table and vomited on the floor.

"Mildred!" Edra grabbed a wet cloth and handed it to Mildred. "Here."

While she wiped her face, Mildred noticed brown particles in the slimy green bile. She quickly bent to clean the floor before Edra noticed but was not quick enough. She remembered the last time they saw something similar. Three days before Sadie's death from intestinal cancer, she had vomited up copious amounts of what looked like coffee grounds. Mildred knew this was blood that came from the stomach. The Bell family with its influential connections spared Sadie no procedure to determine that she had advanced abdominal cancer. The hospital in Carson City had a pathologist trained by Rudolf Virchow who recognized the cells once they were removed by a surgeon and placed on a slide. Sadie was given six months to live after her diagnosis was made. She lasted eight, which was something that neither she nor her family appreciated, since the last three months of her life were spent in excruciating pain and endless bouts of vomiting.

"Mildred, I'm worried about you."

"Don't be. It's just my monthly curse come around again too soon."

"But the specks of blood?"

"Oh that…had a little nose bleed last night. All the dry weather …probably swallowed some blood." She didn't mention it did concern her that it could be something worse. Nor did she mention all the pressure she'd felt lately. It was better to suppress the worry than risk upsetting Edra further, despite the toll it was taking on her.

"The vomiting?"

"You know that happens with me sometimes."

Edra knew that was true. She had seen Mildred's bloody nose the night before and didn't want to push this any further. "You'd tell me if something was wrong?"

"Yes."

＊

Since Charley started feeling better he went out to the Whitmore's place to spend more time with Mabel and little Frankie. He loved throwing the ball for Cranky and watching him tumble over himself trying to fetch it. "Good boy. Bring the ball back!" he yelled as the dog headed in the opposite direction. He laughed at the vision of Mabel trying to coax the ball away from Cranky. He'd throw that ball till they were all exhausted, Cranky panting and circling to find the right spot to rest, Mabel down in her bed next to the baby's crib, and he'd go home to his own and fall into a deep peaceful sleep, to return the next day and they'd go at it again. He even insisted that Frank and Helene take time off from the kids, offering to watch them.

On this particular day they took him up on the offer and went to town, Frank to catch up on chores at the blacksmith, while Helene met up with Sarah and Josie for afternoon tea.

"He's there today. Came around yesterday. I couldn't believe my ears when he said he wanted to babysit the kids." Helene smiled.

Sarah's ears perked up.

"And so where's Mildred?" Josie entered in with sarcasm. "Told you."

Helene became defensive. "Told us what?"

"He's no sooner interested in her than I am," she laughed. "Perish the thought he'd have anything to do with that witch."

"But, Charley seems happy. He was even singing yesterday." Helene did not want to hear anything that would put a damper on her plans to get Charley and Mildred together and get closer to some of her money.

"What's he so happy about? Don't you think it's fishy? One minute in love, then devastated, and before we snap our fingers he's hanging with the ugliest curse in Red River Pass? Come on now. He's got something on his mind. No way he's attracted to that pig."

That annoyed Sarah. "Maybe not!"

Josie replied with indignation. "When am I ever wrong?"

Sarah and Helene bit their tongues.

"When have you known me to be mistaken? I know what I see. I'm not stupid."

"Hey, come on," said Helene nervously.

Sarah put in her two cents. "Yeah, no need to get in a huff over this. What're you getting all worked up over anyway?"

"Worked up? I'm not worked up! Just cause I call it like it is. She doesn't deserve her papa's money. They got no class to their name to claim all that money..."

"But her mamma..."

"Her mamma didn't bring a lick of money into that relationship. So what if she was a Bell. She married beneath her. Lost any class she had when she took up with Max Dunlap. They don't deserve spit! I'm more deserving than them." Josie stopped herself from saying more. *None of you would understand anyway. What could you possibly know about having a name, coming from good stock?* Painful memories weren't worth sharing where they'd never be understood.

Helene was bewildered. "Whatever are you talking about?"

The edge left Josie's voice. "Never mind."

"Well, I don't care about the reason. I'm out enjoying myself and have me a babysitter. I see nothing bad in any of that. Come on, Josie, let's just enjoy our tea." Helene reached for a cookie.

Sarah commented, "Could there be something with him and Mildred?"

Quick as a knee jerk, Josie's attitude resurfaced. "That unsociable hag. She's too plain ugly. Look how she dresses. Why, with all her money you'd think she'd try to at least look better. Wearing all those plain Sears and Roebuck things. She could afford better. She's a pitiful shame of an excuse for a woman. She does nothing with her hair either." Josie compared her attire with Mildred's, how she prided herself in dressing elegantly in heavy satin with decorated neck, hem, and gored seams on her skirts. She dressed well at the expense of her family going without. She enjoyed feeling superior to Mildred in fashion. "She's not even wearing the latest puffed sleeves. I bet she doesn't even wear a corset. Lets all her flab just hang." She laughed about the lack in Mildred's taste: no braids, puffs, frills, gathers, tucks, pleats, or fancy collars. "She can afford better and what does she do? Buys cotton!" She waved a hand over the material of her dress to make her point, then brushed a few curls back into a wave that met a chignon at the back of her neck.

"Who cares? Charley is perking up!" Helene finished chewing on the cookie. "And I'm pleased as Punch."

"Sure, Helene. Why should you care if there's something evil going on?" Josie looked at Sarah. "And you, I suppose you agree with Helene."

"Me?" Sarah sounded intimidated. "No, Josie. I see your point."

Josie said, "How come if he likes Mildred so much he's spending time with your kids? Something's wrong with that picture. Charley is up to no good with that fat hog."

Helene cowered. "I don't think so."

"Josie does have a point, Helene. How come he is spending more time at your place and not with Mildred?"

Helene nervously reached for another vanilla cookie and took a bite. "That's delicious. You'll have to give me the recipe."

"Helene!" Josie exclaimed, demanding an answer.

Helene desperately wanted to get Josie off her back. The force with her words was all too painfully familiar. If her past taught her anything it taught her it was easier to capitulate then face the consequences of an escalation. The more she resisted, the greater the force used by her father, and now she was feeling a similar gut-wrenching as Josie's words poured over her. "Well," Helene paused. "He did tell me..."

Sarah interrupted, "What?"

Josie slashed in. "Let her finish!"

Helene continued, "Mildred has that situation with Edra. You know. And neither one of them has friends going out there. Charley has to take it easy till he hears from Mildred so Edra doesn't get upset."

Josie and Sarah watched Helene eat one more cookie and sip her tea. "Anything else?" asked Josie.

"He did say that Ben told him they're doing some big construction project on the barn."

Josie asked, "What the heck does that have to do with Mildred and Charley?"

"Mildred oversees projects," Helene replied and grabbed for the last cookie.

Josie became outraged. "Why does she have to have her nose in every little thing, with all her money? Why doesn't she let others just do their jobs? I can't stomach that woman!"

"That Edra is all messed up. I'd want to keep busy with other things too," Sarah agreed.

"All that money! She could get someone out there to help Edra. Lots of good folk could use some work. Mildred is a selfish wicked woman."

Helene did not say another word.

*

When Charley returned home that night, he found the note that Ben had left attached to his front door.

The next day, Charley took his buggy out to Mildred's place. He arrived a little early and was greeted by Edra. "Have a seat, Charley." She pointed to the bench on the front porch. "I'll go tell Mildred you're here."

Mildred was in the bedroom still dressing. She had put on a plain black cotton dress with a full skirt that went from mid-neck to her ankles. She wore extra petticoats in case the pads did not absorb the bleeding. Cramping in her belly was causing nausea and she hoped she could keep her breakfast down. As she stood at the mirror to arrange her hair, she noticed that she looked pale. A little rouge on her cheeks took care of that. When she was ready, she went to the porch and greeted Charley. "Glad you could come."

"Good to see you. Was wondering if you'd like to take a ride out to see Zach Langford with me?"

"All the way to Walker Junction?"

"Yeah, he has a horse he wants me to take a look at before he offers it to someone else. Good price. We could grab a bite there…"

87

"I don't know, Charley. That's an awful long time to be away. I need to make dinner for Edra."

"Edra can come along."

Edra, hearing her name, went back onto the porch in a supportive show for Mildred. "Did I hear my name?"

"I was just telling Mildred it'd be fine for you to come along with us to Walker Junction."

"No." Edra shook her head. "No."

Mildred looked at Charley, begging sympathy. "Charley, I better not. Maybe you can just stay a while now then go to Zach's yourself?"

"Why sure, if that's what you'd like."

"Think it'd be best." She turned to Edra. "Would you mind making some tea?"

Edra nodded.

"So tell me, are you thinking of getting another horse?"

They made small talk while Edra fixed the tea. They talked about the horse, Charley's doing some carpenter work for the school, and spending time out at the Whitmore's. When Edra returned, they had tea and continued the light banter till he left.

Mildred went in to find Edra folding laundry. "That wasn't too bad."

Edra put a pile of clothes into a drawer. "True."

"If we can just stay the course, we'll be okay."

"That's a funny expression. Never heard you use it before."

Mildred tried to remember where she'd seen it. Then it dawned on her it was in the play she read by Marlow based on the Faust story, about a man who sells his soul to the devil. She found it metaphorically telling that she would use this now and wondered if the nightmares and physical changes were a result of her selling her soul by compromising her integrity. Was something being revealed she needed to pay attention to? And, if so, was it too late to do anything about it? Or would she have time, like the deal Faustus struck with Lucifer, before the axe fell? *Have I damned myself to hell?* "It's from that play I read a while back. You didn't want to read it."

"What's it mean?"

"Continue to pursue the goal despite criticisms or barriers."

Edra smiled. "That sure says it."

"You seem to be sitting easier with this now."

"Well, today's a pretty okay day. So, for right now…" Edra laughed, "I can say yeah."

"Man is least himself when he talks in his own person. Give him a mask, and he will tell you the truth." OSCAR WILDE

13

Charley lived on the north side of town, around the corner and just down the side street from Gus Spivey's General Store. His home sided the small wood schoolhouse that he, with several others, helped build. He loved to put his carpentry trade to use to help children, and before Emma took ill often stopped by the school to assist with odd jobs. Although he didn't spend much of his time reading, he enjoyed helping the children after school with theirs.

The morning after his visit to Mildred's, he awoke, looked out the window of his one-bedroom house to the empty schoolyard, and envisioned children running and giggling, playing tag, jump rope, and hopscotch. *Mildred Dunlap, you sure were smart to bring Mabel around that first time.* He dressed, put on his hat, and made his way up the street. As he turned the corner, he found Gus opening his store.

"Morning, Gus."

Gus smiled. "Hey, Charley. On your way to church?"

"Yes. Too bad you have to keep shop on Sundays. You'd sure be welcome."

"Mighty nice of you to say so, Charley. You know how it goes with running a business. Somebody has to do it." Gus feigned a laugh.

Charley figured that Gus stayed open for the few travelers passing through in need of food, drink, or emergency supplies. He continued down Main Street where most of the stores were closed.

Men and women in their Sunday best, little girls in their patent leather shoes, and little boys in bowties filed into the church on the south end of town. A slight breeze blowing through the open windows failed to cool off the July heat and stuffy interior.

Amos Jenkins stood before the congregation and took a breath. He had been the minister of the Red River Pass Protestant Church for the past eleven years, sent by a sister church on the east coast after the previous minister, Crayton Miller, had died of measles. Crayton had put the congregation to sleep with his boring sermons, and the townsfolk were glad when new blood arrived. Amos filled the pews and did not disappoint.

The Jenkins were a handsome family. Amos and Rebecca had three children full of life and fun who attended services on Sunday.

Amos looked at his family sitting in the second row and smiled. "Let's talk." Still smiling, his eyes ran over the congregation nodding or mumbling their hellos, being sure to include everyone. "I am smiling, but some of you may not when I tell you what I am going to talk about today."

The room hushed, but for a few younger restless children.

"Death." He paused. "Why do the smiles go out of you when I say that word? Look at you. Look around at the person next to you. Yes, death. It is coming to each and every one of us. And we sit here afraid of it."

Several coughs erupted. A boy sneezed. Handkerchiefs were raised to wipe sweaty foreheads. Adult voices hushed up the young ones. All eyes gazed forward.

"Was Jesus afraid? What can we learn from that day when he walked to his death for us?" He paused, took a deep breath, and glanced around with a peacefulness that put the crowd at ease. He was lit up with a gift, a knowing that words can't touch on the actual. Like a painting representing its subject, words were representations. He compensated with his demeanor, attitude, gestures, which spoke volumes where language fell short. He knew that the best he could do was to point at what he was trying to say and use his speech wisely in an attempt to get through to the hearts of his congregation. "In those darkest hours…what do we see?" He looked over to a wall on the right side of the church at a painting showing Jesus on the cross. "Look at the peaceful expression on his face. What is that?" He knew that a pause for silence was more effective than continuing, so he stood looking at the painting until the room went silent with him. When you could hear a piece of paper drop, he continued, "The light shines on the darkness. It shines within. Always. Look at his eyes…at his darkest moment…there's that spark."

A coughing child caught the attention of his mother. "Shhhh."

Amos waited for the child to gain composure before continuing. "The light within…" He went on to preach about hope as long as one has faith in God, that in our darkest hours the light of God shines within to see us through. He talked about death as a metaphor and not just of the flesh, that all things pass and are impermanent. "All things except the light within…it shines on the darkness. Fear not. Have faith." He raised his voice. "God is always with us. Faith be with you! God be with you!" He had barely taken a breath while delivering his message.

A woman in the back screamed, "Praise God!" Then another, until the entire room joined in. "Praise God!" Mouths were agape, eyes wide open, and attention no longer distracted by the hot stuffy room.

He felt energized by the cheers.

There were more scattered calls of "Praise God!"

Just then a yellow warbler flew in through an open window, grabbing Amos's attention. He laughed. "Well, look who's come to join us."

A couple of men rose to try to shoo it out.

"Seems that our sermon has concluded."

Laugher erupted.

"Madeline will now play a hymn for us." She pressed the pedal on the pump organ and began playing "Steal Away to Jesus." Some members of the congregation readied themselves to leave. Purses shuffled, hymnals were placed back in their holders, and a child whined he was hungry.

Midway through, Josie nudged Satchel that she wanted to leave. She grabbed hold of their two boys and left with Satchel following. When they got outside she whispered to Satchel, "Why'd they have to play that damn nigger song?"

"What's a nigger, mamma?" Matt, her elder son, asked.

Satchel tightened his grip on her arm and whispered back, "Josie! Not here."

When the hymn came to an end, most of the congregation began to leave. Frank with Helene carrying little Frankie, and Mabel walked up to Josie. Helene asked, "How'd you like that? Wasn't that something?"

"I swear," Josie said under her breath. "Amos has brought that northern nigger influence here. Can't we do better than that?"

Satchel shot Josie a look that said, *Shut up!* Helene stepped back, tightening her hold on little Frankie, grabbed Mabel's hand, and nervously moved on with her family.

Inside the church, Charley waited for everyone to leave. He wanted to stay put and let Amos's words linger. It was the first time he'd been back for a sermon since Emma's death and although he missed her deeply it didn't hurt as much as when she passed. He wondered if that's what Amos meant by what he said, that the light would see you through.

When the aisles were emptied, he walked out and around to the back to Emma's gravesite. He sat down beside the headstone and patted the dirt above where her body was laid to rest. "I miss you," he whispered, feeling the emptiness that he had never experienced through all their years together. "There's a part of me never going to be the same and I ain't never going to love again like with you." Tears flowed freely. The sound of a neighbor's barking dog caught his attention. "But there's life here. I still got life in me just like that dog." He looked over to where the barking was coming from to see a black dog wagging its tail and taking a treat from its owner.

He glanced up as a breeze fluttered a few greenish-brown needles of the pinyon pine several feet away, the colors contrasting against the gentle blue sky. As he looked at the other graves, he thought of all the lives that had come and gone, the sorrow that their deaths had brought to those who loved them, and his memories flooded in. He remembered when he first met Emma at a dance. To him, she was the most beautiful woman he'd ever set eyes on, and it seemed too good to be true that after several dates she liked him just as much as he liked her. He remembered the sorrow they felt over him being unable to get her pregnant, the joy they shared with their beloved dog Slappy, and how they had come to name him that. *He'd never do nothing without our slapping our hands to get his attention. What a silly dog. We had so many good years together, my darling Emma.*

Charley inhaled a deep breath, feeling the tears dripping onto his suit jacket. Pausing to listen to the rustle of the trees as the wind became stronger, he observed the dust kick up and tumbleweeds scatter about, while the neighbor's dog across the street sat watching him. He felt a part of life. Even in his sorrow he was glad to be alive, unexpectedly grateful. He patted the grave and said, "I'll be getting on now. I'll come back tomorrow. I love you, my Emma."

*

As Mildred and Edra sat together on their front porch bench, Mildred said, "Those flowers are so beautiful." She pointed to the desert brickell-bush that grew along the sides of the porch. "And I sure love our view of the rolling hills." She sounded nostalgic.

"Sundays are calm," said Edra. "Love our sermon from the birds. That's church enough for me."

Mildred nodded her agreement.

"I wouldn't want to be around all those busybodies and gossips sitting in church right now anyway!" Edra raised her voice.

Mildred moved closer to her. "How you really doing?"

"Truth be told? I don't want to upset you…"

"Go on."

"I wish we could undo the whole thing. Wish we could just move and start all over," moaned Edra. "I still think Charley's showing too much interest in you and I don't like…"

"We've been through this before. You know how I feel about that. Besides, where would we go? Where would we ever be free to just be ourselves without worrying that someone will see something, make trouble for us, or maybe even worse? Where do we go that we don't take ourselves along? People are no different no matter where we'd go. At least here we have our excuses. Here…we're probably safer here, staying put."

Edra pouted. "You don't want to leave this land. It means more to you than me."

"You know that's not true! I do love this land. If I felt we could find a place where we could be…" Mildred paused and looked straight into Edra's dark green eyes. "You know, if I really believed we could go somewhere and just live simply, I would. I love you that much."

"Well then, can't you just tell Charley you only like him as a friend?" Edra pleaded.

"Oh, Edra." Mildred sighed deeply. "If only it were that easy."

"I just keep hoping…" Edra swatted at a fly buzzing around her face.

Mildred took her hand. "You live in false hope and you open yourself up to be bushwhacked. We need to be smart about what we do." Mildred brought Edra's hand to her lips and kissed it. "I love you so much."

"Oh Mil…I know." Edra paused. "I know you're right. I'm sorry I keep bringing this up. I want to be supportive but…it's so hard for me to…"

"You bring it up to me as much as you want if it makes you feel any better."

"What about you? I determine I'm going to be strong for you, then two days later I'm a mess again."

"Oh honey, you know I'm a strong woman. As long as we have each other, we'll just keep holding each other up." Mildred knew it was best not to mention how exhausted she felt.

Edra's attention became distracted.

"Where'd you wander off to?" asked Mildred.

"Look at that spider web." Edra pointed to a messy looking web with a long-legged marbled cellar spider applying a white silk to a captured deer fly. "That poor fly."

"Probably the same one you tried to kill just a few seconds ago." Mildred laughed, releasing a flow of blood between her legs.

"It is absurd to divide people into good and bad. People are either charming or tedious." OSCAR WILDE

14

The ennui of late summer had set into Red River Pass along with the unbearable heat. Mildred had sent a note with Ben to Charley, which said Edra was not well and she needed to tend to her. These things take their time, she wrote and begged his patience. Charley took kindly to it and occupied his time with odd jobs and tending to the children after school. This not only served to calm down things with Mildred and Edra but it helped to play out the stories, rampant in town, of Mildred and Charley's picnic at the lake and their meal at the cafe. No new telegrams of note had arrived to stir up the town in these several weeks, so Satchel was glad when the news came in. He arrived home shortly after five in a very good mood. Josie greeted him at the front door.

"Hey, Satchel. Shorty brought us a present today…" She was interrupted by laughter from her two boys emanating from their bedroom. "Finish your chores, boys!" she yelled. Placing her attention back to Satchel, she said, "Guess who gets to clean up after Shorty?"

Shorty acquired his name from Satchel, when a cousin who came through on a visit two summers ago gave the cat to him and told him he was an American shorthair. The Purdues loved him for his hunting prowess that reduced the rodents in the house. Although he needed no

coaxing, Josie egged him on to catch, torment, and kill the mice popu-
lation invading their place. Get 'em, Shorty! When Shorty caught a
mouse and let it drop, she'd demanded, *Pick it up! Kill it!* When the cat
had complied with her command, he was generously rewarded with
treats. She was proud of Shorty, particularly since she knew his ances-
tors came to America on the *Mayflower*, which gave her bragging rights
to lord it over friends who she professed had *measly strays*. Josie looked
at the dead mouse on the floor in the living room and smiled. "That's
my good boy. Now clean it up, Satchel."

"Here, take a look at these," he said as he waved a couple of
telegrams he was holding. He knew he risked upsetting her over the
news, especially the one about a Negro, but he also knew that if he did
not bring the telegrams home first, she would be all over him. He was
sure that the news about Booker T. Washington's Atlanta Address was
going to infuriate her. He was well aware of her view on Negroes being
allowed to succeed, that it should never have happened, let alone have
them gain any sovereignty. He never understood why she had such an
aversion to people of color, but after broaching the subject with her
several times, only to be shut down, he gave up asking about it. What he
hoped was that the other telegram, about the Jew in France, would dull
the impact.

Satchel held out the first telegram.

Josie grabbed it out of his hand and said, "Now, go clean up that
critter."

She began to read. "Are you kidding me! Has this been posted at
Gus's yet?"

"Not yet." Satchel knelt and scooped up the dead mouse with a
small hand spade.

She continued reading about Washington's Atlanta Address, which
highlighted his extremely charismatic nature, a magnet for people of
wealth and power. It said he was a representative of the last generation
of black leaders who had been born into slavery. "All those rich white
folk supporting that man! Why he's no better than any other slave. A
black slave mamma and a white man! They should have drowned him

when he was born! God damn them all to hell!" she screamed, then threw the telegram to the floor and ran out the back door.

Satchel ran after her and found her leaning into a tall tree crying her eyes out.

"Why!" she screamed. "God damn it all to hell! Those no-goods!"

"Josie, calm yourself. Come back in the house," he pleaded.

"Leave me alone!"

"You're gonna scare the children."

"Let 'em get scared. Might do some good to teach 'em what happens when you're nice to scum. They creep in and take over, rob everybody…"

"What are you talking about? You're not making any sense. So what if…"

"So what?" she screamed. "Are you crazy?"

"Okay, calm down. What's gotten into you? You were in such a good mood when I came home. Pull yourself together."

"I will not!"

"You will when you see this next one. Jew boy in France got his." He held up the telegram.

That got her attention. "Give me that." She grabbed it out of his hand. "My eyes are blurry." She reached into the pocket of his pants to get his handkerchief, wiped her eyes, and began reading.

Satchel was relieved her flare-ups were short-lived.

She smiled. "Oh this is good."

She read about Alfred Dreyfus, a French artillery officer of Jewish background, whose trial and conviction in Paris on charges of treason was becoming one of the most sensational political dramas in French history. He was a graduate of the elite École Polytechnique Military School at Fontainebleau. When a highly placed spy passed new artillery information to the Germans, widespread anti-Semitism in French society, particularly in the conservative military, threw suspicion onto Dreyfus. He became a target of the French Army's counter-intelligence section, and was arrested for treason in October 1894. On the fifth of January 1895, he was summarily convicted in a secret court martial,

99

publicly stripped of his army rank, and sentenced to life imprisonment. Josie was in glee till she came to the part about Dreyfus's possible innocence being leaked to the French press. "What! That has to be a lie. Who'd come to a Jew's defense?" Her laughter ceased as she read out loud, "…resulting in a heated debate on anti-Semitism, France's identity as a Catholic nation, and a republic founded on equal rights for all citizens…" She crushed the paper in her hand. "They won't let him get away with it. I know he has to be guilty. Can't trust those kind…it's his fault anyway. Why'd he have to go to that elite school? Should know his place. These people are so stupid."

Satchel responded. "He should stay in prison and learn his lesson."

Josie smiled and Satchel felt comforted that he had succeeded in breaking the tension.

*

The next day, after Charley had finished helping the kids at school, he made his way to Gus's store to pick up a few things for his supper. There was still a crowd gathered around the noticeboard, carrying on like there was no tomorrow, which annoyed Gus.

"What's all that about?" Charley asked Gus.

"Some news came in about a religious scandal in France. Catholic Church against Jews." Gus lowered his voice. "All our good Protestants here think they're holier than…"

"I've got a shopping list here," interrupted Charley, as he ignored what Gus said and handed him his list.

"And some Negro has them all up in arms."

Charley noticed the sarcasm in Gus's tone, which was unusual.

Gus took the list from Charley. "You eating alone tonight, Charley?"

"Yes. Just get me a couple things here and I'll make myself a little something."

"I'm going to clear the place out early. How's about sticking around to share a meal with me? I've got plenty."

"That's a darn nice offer. Don't mind if I do."

Gus ushered everybody out as fast as he could and closed up shop.

In the flat above the store where he lived, Gus prepared a meal while Charley sat and relaxed with a shot glass of whiskey. Charley looked around at the cozy flat. A single bed stood against the far wall next to a small bookcase, and on the other side of the room near the table where Charley was sitting was a wood-burning stove and cabinet with dishes. A dusty worn Persian rug rested on the wood plank floor underneath the table, something Gus must have ordered along with his other international items, Charley guessed. There were boxes scattered about with books stacked on them and a partially opened file cabinet spilling its overly stuffed contents. On the wall hung recent news articles that had been clipped from magazines.

"Here you go." Gus placed two plates of meat and fried potatoes on the table.

They sat quietly as they ate until Gus broke the silence, "That crowd today. I tell you there are some days I'd just as soon pick up and go live alone somewhere else. Got some hermit blood in me." He downed his third shot glass of whiskey.

"Gus, you're one of the most social guys in town. We'd sure hate to ever see you move on."

"I have to be. I own a store." He downed a fourth shot. "Another?" He held up the whiskey bottle.

"No more for me, thanks."

"Church people all riled up about some poor Jewish kid. People hating Negroes just cause of the color of their skin. All this bullshit because a Jew got some rank and status and a Negro got wealth and power. Big joke. Our little townsfolk think they're better than them. Why? Religious people thinking others are inferior if they don't hold the same views. It just don't make any sense to me. Where's God in all this?"

"It's really bothering you?" Charley asked, sensing that something was eating away at Gus.

"This is why I don't like to go to church. No offense, Charley. I like everyone all right. Things might have been different if I married and had kids. It's different when you have to give the little ones some foundation." He gulped down another shot.

Charley noticed that Gus had begun to slur his words.

"I tell you, to be honest Charley, I ain't got no stomach for churches. What do they teach you? Hatred? Blame someone else? Make someone wrong because they don't have your skin color, your bloodline, or your same beliefs? I'll tell you what I believe, Charley, that we can't get answers. That Bible is a story. Like any other book. How come people are so in love with that story? I don't see God in any book. I don't see God in hatred or thinking someone is less than you. I'm not less than anyone!" Gus's speech was bordering on incomprehensible. "I'll jes ha masef a lil more." He grabbed the bottle.

"I think you may have had enough there."

Gus pulled himself together. "Never enough. There ain't enough booze in the world to shut my mind to what I feel is just plain wrong!" Gus was completely unaware of how loud he was becoming.

"Maybe you could go over and talk with Amos? Seems like a decent enough fellow."

"I ain't talking to no one from any church. Why, my mother would quake in her grave." Gus knew that even in his inebriated state he had let slip something he'd never intended. He managed to catch himself and back down. "I'm okay, Charley. You've been so kind to listen to me. Hope my big mouth didn't turn you off. Don't mean nobody any harm. You know me, good old Gus." He looked at Charley with bloodshot eyes and smiled, drool oozing down his chin.

"Don't be worrying about anything you say to me, Gus. I wouldn't cause no trouble to come to you. Got enough of it myself with people asking about me and Mildred."

"She's not a bad soul. Nice thing you got someone. Nice thing. I'm happy for you, Charley."

"Well Gus, think it's time for some shut eye. Sure did enjoy the meal and our chat."

"Sure thing. Let me see you down."

Charley stood to leave.

Gus stumbled as he tried to stand.

Charley motioned for him to sit. "I'll find my way out. Thanks again."

"We'll be seeing ya," slurred Gus before he nodded off.

Two hours later he came to and readied himself for bed, but before he went to sleep that night, he pulled up a floorboard under his bed and took out a small metal box. Inside was an object wrapped neatly in a handkerchief. He unwrapped and kissed it. Gus rarely took out the box with the tiny object in it that his mother gave him. It would have been too dangerous. People were persecuted and killed because of it, and so he hid his mezuzah.

Gus's family had changed their name when they came to America. The only thing his mother retained of her heritage was the tiny mezuzah that her parents had given her. She withheld knowledge of its existence until she lay on her deathbed. It was then she called her twelve-year-old son to her bedside and removed the mezuzah that she had kept hidden in her bust. It was still wrapped in the same cloth as when her parents gave it to her. "Gus, this is something I never told you about," she said to the boy. "I never wanted to subject you to the hatred my parents witnessed in Russia. They were Jewish." She went on to tell him of the horrors the Jews were subjected to. She handed him the tiny wrapped article. "It contains a piece of parchment scroll on which are written certain Biblical passages. Take it. Keep it safe. Protect yourself, my son."

"Mamma," he said, pointing to a name inscribed on the cover of the tiny wood container, "what's this?"

"That is the name of God," she gasped. "Keep it safe. Never allow hatred to fill your heart. That will only hurt you." He saw the light fading from her eyes. These were Miriam's last words.

"A little sincerity is a dangerous thing, and a great deal is absolutely fatal." — Oscar Wilde

15

Two weeks passed since the telegrams arrived. In the interim, Mildred sent another note to Charley saying that Edra was still fragile, a feigned excuse she was comfortable continuing to tell him, and that she would let him know when they could resume their visits. With word from Ben that the town's gossip had calmed, she began to regain her equanimity. Once the commotion, the overwhelming stimulation, quieted down, her body started to heal: the heavy vaginal bleeding reduced to irregular spotting, the nausea and lack of appetite resolved, and color returned to her cheeks. The time away from Charley and town was exactly what she needed. It also helped that it afforded Edra's anxiousness an opportunity to lessen and take a back seat. Once she regained her strength she decided she needed to resume forward motion on the plan. The fact that Lil's hind shoe was loose gave Mildred the perfect excuse to return to town to have it fixed and drop in on Charley.

"Think it's time I head back to town. Lil's shoe needs fixing." Mildred watched carefully for any reaction in Edra and seeing none continued, "Also think I'll pay Charley a visit."

Edra flushed. "Oh, you sent him a note?"

"No, just thought I'd drop by his place. I don't have to if you…"

"No. It just took me a little by surprise." She didn't want to stir

Mildred up. They had spent so much time unwinding, talking, starting to feel better, and had talked about resuming the visits but Edra assumed it would be out at the ranch. She knew Mildred was getting antsy about making excuses in notes back to Charley but didn't want to face the time had come, still worried how things would play out. "You're right. Glad we had this time together. It's sure helped. Go on now."

Everyone in town was exhausted with stories about the Negro and the Jew, stories that by now had been blown way out of proportion. Unsuspecting, Mildred arrived at Pursey Funkle's Blacksmith Shop around lunchtime, and met up with Pursey who was having a sandwich.

"Hey there Mildred, been a long time." Pursey wiped a few crumbs off the side of his mouth.

"Sorry to interrupt your lunch. I'll just have a seat over here and wait till you're done." She moved toward a bench outside the entrance when Pursey motioned for her to stay inside.

"It's no bother at all. Have a seat here if you like." He patted a chair next to where he was sitting. "I have an extra apple if you haven't eaten yet."

Mildred, feeling very uncomfortable and suspicious of his motives, took the seat. "Thank you, but I ate just before coming out."

"Sarah's home with a bit of a bug. Upset stomach. Truth is I think she's been running around too much. Having teas, visiting with the ladies in town. Too much excitement."

Mildred nodded with a smile.

"Yeah, I tell you there's no end to the commotion when news comes in. People getting rich just because they can stand in front of a crowd. They don't have to do a lick of work, just talk and people with money, lots of money, take to them like flies to dung. You'd think a Negro would know what it means to sweat. All that talk over getting their kind into schools."

Mildred looked confused.

Pursey took the last bite of his sandwich then pulled one of the two apples out of his bag. "You sure?" He held the apple out to Mildred.

"Yes, very kind of you."

He took a bite, then attempted to speak but instead spewed acrid-smelling spittle mixed with bits of apple into the air, catching Mildred's face. "Pardon, my excitement." He held out a napkin to her.

Mildred, repulsed, used it to clean her cheek.

"What do you think of all these goings on?"

She was perplexed. "I'm not really sure."

"Why Mildred, have you even heard the latest?" It finally dawned on him that maybe she had not.

"I've not been around that much lately."

"Why, you don't know!"

He lapsed into a monologue of exaggerated details, altered beyond original description: The Negro must have lied, probably has some rich white women sponsoring him because he's good in bed, and the Jew deserved to be imprisoned for having the gall to try to become something he was not born into. "People should know their place. When they are made by God to be inferior, they should just do their best to stay out of the way of the good hard-working folk who are the backbone of society."

Mildred was disgusted. Anger welled up into her throat that wanted to be let out in a scream and she felt an urge to pick up one of the horse-shoes and whack him to shut him up. As the blood began draining from her head, she felt sick to her stomach. "Oh my," she mumbled, trying to ease out of the tirade.

He kept on and on, discharging a hatred that gave her chills. She knew then and there, beyond any doubt, that the fear she had felt when she first heard of Oscar Wilde's conviction was not just about prejudice existing across a continent and ocean, but rather the ignorance that lives in closed minds everywhere. The seeds that grow and inflate the smallest minds into giants, those who believe they can take down anyone with their petty realities, was what she saw full-blown in Pursey. It mattered not whether his reality was based on prejudice, fear, or just plain ignorance, the end result would be the same, ruined lives. The tone in his voice reminded her of Josie that day outside the telegraph office. She now understood why up till that time this sort of talk didn't bother her.

The hatred was now something personal and she knew, no matter the excuses, that she and Edra no longer were immune from suspicion.

These were realities, as sure as the loose shoe on Lil's hoof, as painful as the belly cramps now gripping and sending spasms of bile into her throat, and the strained effort to breathe. This reality was something she knew she would have to live with for the rest of her life—that where closed minds live, she and Edra could never be free.

She tried to settle the pain swelling up inside her gut while she listened to Pursey chewing loudly on his apple. She could no more control her insides than she could stop the blacksmith shop from spinning around her.

Pursey ran to get a damp cloth while he yelled to Sam Larue who was passing by, "Go get Doc Nichols! Mildred just passed out!"

*

When Mildred came to, she found herself on a bed in Doc Nichols' home with Charley sitting by her side. Still nauseous, head pounding, she pulled at her dress that had stuck to her chest with moisture. She could hear Doc talking with a patient in another room. She tried to speak but words would not come.

Charley brushed a cool damp cloth across her forehead. "Well, there you are." He helped her take a sip of water.

"Charley." She barely got the word out of her parched mouth.

"You gave us a scare. Here, have some more water." He handed her the glass. She gazed up at him, still dazed. He put the water glass in her hand and helped her drink it. He watched her and saw innocence, a beauty that vulnerability brings, and he knew he was sharing something very sensitive with Mildred. He felt sorrow, for the last time he was in this room was with Emma, just before she took to her bed. He also felt somewhat responsible, that in wanting to cultivate this friendship he brought the town's attention onto her. He wished people would shut up and leave her alone. He felt the same when Emma took ill, shut them up and shut them out, shut out everything but hope, until all became hopeless and he wanted to die, and then Mildred had changed that for him. Now he wished he could repay the favor. "You passed out over at

107

Pursey's. Doc and Sam Larue carried you here. Doc says you were moaning about someone, something about someone doing something bad. I came as soon as I heard."

Doc Nichols entered the room. "How you feeling?" He moved closer to her noticing her facial pallor, dark circles under her eyes, dry skin, rapid breathing, which were all signs of shock. He took her hand. "Let me check your hydration." He took a fold of skin from the palmar surface of her hand and pinched some skin between his fingers. It stayed tented. "Just what I thought." He put her hand down.

"What is it, Doc?" asked Charley.

Doc asked Mildred, "How much water have you been drinking?"

She mumbled, "Not sure…"

"I can tell you this," he looked over at Charley then back to Mildred, "it's not enough. You're dehydrated."

Mildred felt her soaked clothes clinging to her body and knew she must have perspired a lot of fluid in the heat while Pursey ranted. She also knew she did need to drink more water.

"Will she be okay?"

Doc smiled at them. "Should be. Make sure you drink more, rest up…I'll also give you something to help your iron in case that might be contributing to how pale you look."

"Okay," she replied.

"Charley will see you home."

"I can manage."

"Not a good idea. You take it easy now."

"Lil?"

Charley answered. "Her shoe's fixed. We'll get her and hook her to my buggy. I'll go get her and be right back."

When he walked out Doc asked Mildred, "Anything else going on with you that you want to tell me about?"

She thought this over and decided it best to refrain from anything further. "Not really. I'll pay better attention to drinking more water. With the heat and all…"

"Don't hesitate to let me know if you need anything."

Under a near full moon, which cast an eerie light upon the stillness of the night, they made it back to her place. The minute Edra saw Charley with Mildred at the front door, she knew something was terribly wrong. She contained the panic she felt as she helped Mildred in and said good-bye to Charley. As the night progressed and cricket sounds grew louder, Lil neighed and paced, her instincts telling her that Mildred was in trouble.

"Most modern calendars mar the sweet simplicity of our lives by reminding us that each day that passes is the anniversary of some perfectly uninteresting event." OSCAR WILDE

16

Charley entered Gus's store feeling dejected. He wished he could do more to help Mildred but saw when he took her home the night before and spoke with Edra, it would be best to just let things be. He offered to help Edra assist Mildred to her bedroom but Edra insisted, with a force that surprised him, that he wait where he was, on the porch. As he watched Mildred being assisted by Edra, he wondered why they never invited him into their home. He also contemplated how suddenly things can change; one minute Mildred was vivacious, the next she passed out, and although he felt for certain the heat played a part in her spell, he was reminded that nothing is forever nor for certain, and sooner or later life is going to hand you tough breaks.

Gus took one look at Charley and felt guilty. "Hope all my drinking didn't...I'm sorry if I...I never learn..."

Charley took note of the shame Gus was showing. "Don't worry about it."

Just then a customer moved into earshot of them, and Gus immediately switched the conversation. "I was just looking at this here." He showed Charley the catalogue he was holding. "The latest women's bicycling outfits."

"Pants? Never seen nothing like that before." Charley tried to make light conversation in spite of the heaviness pressing in on him from lack of sleep. He had tossed and turned the night before, replaying his conversation with Edra when she came out from helping Mildred, slouched and ashen.

"Thank you, Charley. She just needs to get some rest now."

"That's what Doc said. Said she needs to drink…"

"Yes, Charley, Mildred told me."

"And he gave her something for her iron."

"Charley, thank you. Now I need to…"

"Anything else I can do for you?"

"Not that I can think of. Thanks again for getting her home safely."

He interrupted her attempt to turn to the door. "How about I come back tomorrow to see how…help out with anything if…"

"We'll be all right. Think it's better if we just let her rest without…"

"I understand. I just wanted to…you'll need shopping…"

She showed impatience. "It's getting late, Charley."

"You'll let me know if you need anything?"

"We'll get word to you."

Lost in his thoughts, Charley had not noticed that Gus had shelved new supplies and that quite a while had passed before he heard a couple of women by the public noticeboard speaking in excited voices.

"They've got him on a treadmill six hours a day." The reference was to the latest news on Wilde's imprisonment.

"That's too good for him. Lock him in a cell and throw away the key!"

The women passed Charley and went out the door, leaving a few stragglers in the near empty store.

Gus was concerned that Charley was just standing around and not shopping, which was unusual. "Something I can do for you, Charley?"

"Just trying to think about dinner tonight," he said in a sad tone.

Gus muttered self-consciously, "You sure my mouthing off…hope I didn't say nothing off-putting."

"No, nothing to do with that. I should be thanking you again for the meal." Charley mustered up a smile to reassure Gus he meant what he had said.

Two women entered, catching Gus's attention, and he quickly grabbed for the catalogue he had been eyeing earlier.

Charley noted that he changed the subject for their benefit.

"Finally we're getting some practical clothing for women to bicycle in. All the restrictive things they have to wear inhibit their movement when they're riding. These here are bloomers. Started making them decades ago but like most things in life, a battle was fought over their propriety and this cycling craze is gonna change all that."

The women in the store approached Gus to pay for their items. They glanced curiously at the pictures of the bloomers, but were not inclined to be drawn into any discussion. They settled up with Gus and left.

"That true about them bloomers?" Charley smiled.

"Sure thing." Gus smiled back at Charley. "You having dinner with Mildred?"

"Not tonight."

Gus perked up, and clearly relieved, gushed, "If you're not busy later I'm going to cook some chicken with fixings. Be glad to have you join me." Charley hesitated, prompting Gus to continue, "I'm sorry. I guess you don't want another go-around with me."

He did not want to offend Gus, beside which he thought the distraction would do him some good. "Gus, that chicken you're making…you sure you'll have enough for the hungry likes of me?" Charley smiled.

"You bet! How's about coming back after five-thirty when I close?"

"I've got some leftover pie I bought from Barney's place. Apple. I'd be happy to share it."

"Sounds good to me."

As he left the store, Charley ran into little Johnny Nestor with his mother Georgia.

"Mamma, look!"

Georgia smiled down at her boy, then at Charley. "Good to see you, Charley. Johnny's been telling us about all the time you've been spending with him at school. We're sure grateful you're helping out there. Rebecca has her hands full with church and school duties."

Charley affectionately patted the boy on the shoulder. "You got a smart little fellow here. Full of questions. Likes me reading to him. Don't you, Johnny?"

"Sure do."

Charley laughed. "I'll be around tomorrow and I'll be sure to wear my baggy pants." Johnny knew he was referring to him tugging on Charley's pant leg to get his attention.

"Georgia, nice to see you."

"Same here, Charley."

"Bye-bye, Charley." Johnny gave a big smile showing off a bucktooth.

Charley headed out, his mood elevated by his visit with Gus. He was glad to have an invite and looked forward to having someone to talk with later. He was also pleased that he had run into Johnny Nestor and reflected on how refreshing it was to be around children and their honesty. He remembered the meal that he had with Gus and compared that conversation to how he felt around the children and, to his surprise, felt a commonality between the two. Their conversation had been open and unadulterated and he was looking forward to having another meal with a man who did not present the usual boring predictable cackle.

Later that evening as the sun was setting, turning the hillside aglow with a reddish hue, Gus and Charley finished their apple pie. "Look at that." Gus motioned out the window. "That's what the settlers must have seen when they decided to name this place."

"Sure is pretty." Charley saw a trail of smoke coming from the distance. "Someone must be burning waste. Sure hope it don't catch the tinder out there. We're having quite a dry year."

"Yeah." Gus continued looking out the window. "After a hard day, I come up here, throw a hard one down and look at that. That's all I need."

Charley watched as the sun dove down below the horizon, casting a deep pink wave of color that settled over the mountain. He felt full, satisfied, and appreciative for the company. "Looks like a slow river moving over those hills," he said, referring to the sun's movement.

Gus had avoided taking any alcohol during their meal but now that they had finished, offered Charley a shot. "Care for one?"

"Not tonight, Gus."

Still wanting to undo threads of remorse he felt by overdoing it the last time, Gus put his glass down without pouring. "Had things on my mind the other night needed numbing." He nervously laughed.

"Tell you the truth, I enjoyed the evening. Hope you continue to feel free to speak your mind with me." Charley looked down at the empty glasses. "I don't talk much with people. When you get right down to it, what all is there to talk about with most folk around here?"

Gus nodded agreement.

"Seems to me a lot of it is blather, which is either boring or ends up offending. Just not interested in that."

"I agree with you, Charley. Most of what people around here gab about is nonsense and worse. So much going on in the world, so many interesting people, places, history. People around here hunger for news to come in so they can point fingers and inflate themselves at someone else's expense."

"Inflate?"

"Make someone else look inferior makes 'em feel important."

"Oh yeah, that. Wasn't sure what you meant."

Gus continued, "Lot of prejudice. There are so many more interesting things to talk about."

"Like what, Gus?"

Gus looked at a pile of books resting upon a box by the door, a reminder to bring them down to the store where he had set up a lending library. His collection included books from all over the world. "Do you like to read much?"

"I like to read. Most of the reading I do is with the kids after school," Charley laughed. "What you said the other night got me thinking.

About the Bible…"

Gus lowered his head. "I wish I hadn't said some things. I meant no disrespect."

"I'm glad you did."

He looked at Charley. "Really?"

"Never looked at it like it was just a book. I kinda liked having a new perspective. New way of looking at something."

"It's a delicate subject."

"I know that, Gus," he sighed. "I liked listening to something new that got me thinking. I have thoughts too…been afraid to say some of them. What would people think?"

"Amen." Gus oozed sarcasm.

Charley laughed. "Children don't hold back. They just say it like it is. It's refreshing."

"That's the truth."

"You sure have a lot of books there," said Charley.

"Those books up against the wall over there…" Gus pointed to a corner stacked high with books. "Even got one from that Wilde fellow." These were the books Gus would not be adding to the library in the store. They were too controversial.

"Who?" Charley asked, the name not familiar, having been preoccupied with Emma's death at the time the news had broken of Oscar Wilde.

"A writer. Lives in England. Well, now he's in prison."

"How come?" asked Charley.

"Was caught in the act with another man. The man's father took Wilde to court and won the case. Can't have any of that going on under Queen Victoria's nose," mocked Gus. "The town here was in an uproar when the news came in. You can well imagine." Gus fingered one of the shot glasses in front of him. "Think I'll just have a little now." He poured both full. "Change your mind?"

"Since you poured two, sure."

"Don't worry, if you don't want it, it won't go to waste." He pushed the glass to Charley. "Yeah, I tell you…the slightest bit of news comes in, the hatred flares up again. Now they're at it cause something came in about how the guy's spending his time in prison. Six hours a day on a treadmill."

Charley felt the turn in Gus's attitude when he brought up Wilde and he was aware that Gus took to drink when he was bothered. He wondered what it was. "That who they were talking about when I came in earlier?"

"Here you go." He held up his shot glass to make a toast. "Yes, that's who they were blabbing about. As for me, I...I applaud Oscar Wilde!" He downed the shot.

"How come you think he's something special? A man with another man?" Charley pulled a face. "That don't seem right to me."

"Why? Because he's of the mind to live the life he wants to? Most people are living what they think they should instead of what they want. Before you know it, your life has slipped away and you die miserable. You said you like to look at things in a new way?"

"Yeah."

"You believe in the Bible, Charley?"

"Yes, but what does that have to do with..."

"I don't like to talk religion with anyone, Charley. Have your belief. That's fine with me, but don't hate me because I might not agree with it. Not saying I don't but for conversation sake I like to look at things differently. Did you know that most of our original colonies had governments whose laws were based on religion?"

"No, I didn't know that," replied Charley.

"It's true. The law in many of those colonies called for the execution of people who didn't observe set-down religious practices, like attending church on Sunday."

"Gus, that's hard to believe."

"It's true. I'll loan you the book I read that in."

"No, that's okay."

"Point I'm trying to make...your question about a man with a man? It's not that I think he's special, to use your word, but who are we hurting by being with whomever we want in our own bedroom? And along that line…" He poured himself another and nodded to Charley, "You?"

Charley put a hand over his glass. "I'm good."

"Who's that Negro hurting by talking to crowds, trying to get his race educated? Who are you hurting by talking with me? We're just sharing our thoughts. But I'll tell you, Charley, you mention this conversation to anyone and I'll lose customers."

"I told you, Gus…"

"I know you're not going to say anything. But you know it's true." Gus looked over at the stacks of books. "That's why I read so much. A book isn't going to hurt me. A book isn't going to form some opinion about me that could wreck my life. I learn about so many new and great things from reading. I keep to myself with a good book and a shot of whiskey and I'm right with the world." He went on to tell him about some of the great books he had read over the years, mentioning a few of the ones in his private stack.

Charley raised and stretched his arms. "I'm getting tired. Maybe I could do some reading and we could talk about things together?"

"Want to borrow a book? Dickens, Melville, Cooper, or maybe Shakespeare?" laughed Gus.

Charley went over to the books. "There's so many here."

"Take whatever you want. Bring them back when you're finished."

Charley randomly selected a few books. "Thanks. That'll do me. I better be getting on now."

"Sure thing. Let me see you out."

As they walked downstairs to the door, Charley took an interest in what Gus was saying about the books he loaned him. On his way home, he realized spending time with Gus took his attention off worry about Mildred.

"I always like to know everything about my new friends, and nothing about my old ones." OSCAR WILDE

17

With the news of Mildred's collapse, Josie was invigorated. She had been mouthing off to anyone who'd listen and speculating about why it happened, none of which was favorable. In the middle of tea at Sarah's, she screamed. "She's pregnant!"

Sarah dropped her teacup, spilling tea on the table. Madeline choked on her biscuit. Hanah could not believe her ears. "How do you know that?"

"What else could it be? She's out on a date and then the next time she's in town she faints."

Madeline, still trying to clear her throat of crumbs, attempted to ask, "Do you really think that's…" before she went into coughing spasms.

Hanah got her a glass of water. "Here."

"What else? That woman is healthy as a horse. Why, she even looks like a horse!" Josie laughed.

Sarah cleaned up the spill on the table with her napkin. "But Charley…" she hesitated, "Emma was his love. Everybody knows that. He wouldn't do that."

"He's a man! Get your head out of that fog you're in. Look at all the men trouble this town's been through. Jackson Carrow went out on his wife, didn't he? They were like Charley and Emma, weren't they?" Josie sipped her tea. "Sarah, what kind of tea is this? Mighty tasty."

Madeline continued to cough.

Hanah shook her head. "I just can't believe…"

"Don't have to believe nothing. Just look at it," Josie insisted. "What else could it be? That Mildred is always so secretive. Never comes around to join in with us. Gotta have secrets! She makes me sick with her higher than mighty way. Someday she's gonna get what she deserves…"

Madeline tried to speak up. "But Charley wouldn't…"

"Oh, Charley wouldn't?" Josie slammed back in sarcasm.

"Charley's not Jackson Carrow," said Hanah.

"And?" Josie looked at the women one at a time with a slow movement of her head. "Don't you find it strange that Charley came around from his loss with Emma so fast?"

No one replied.

"Point made," Josie stated with satisfaction.

"Wait till Helene hears this," said Hanah.

"And Pat!" exclaimed Sarah.

"No! We can't tell anyone else," said Josie.

"Why on earth not?" Sarah asked as she poured herself another cup of tea.

"I think we need to figure out a way to pay Mildred a visit. Don't want to alert her we know. You keep this to yourselves!" Josie authoritatively commanded. "Do you hear me?"

"Yeah, sure Josie," Sarah winced.

Josie looked at Madeline and Hanah. They did not respond.

*

Three days had passed since Mildred's episode in town and in that time she rested and let Edra tend to her needs. Edra was having none of Mildred's insistence that what she reacted to was Pursey's barrage coupled with the heat, and told her, "You're still pale."

"I know but it'll take a few days for the medicine to kick in."

"What Doc gave you to boost your iron?

"Yes."

"Have you looked in a mirror?" Edra was worried and on the verge of tears. "Shouldn't it be working by now?"

Mildred knew Edra was right but avoided answering the question. Two nights earlier, she had awakened in a sweat and quietly changed her nightgown hoping she would not wake Edra. She didn't want to talk about what was happening in her body, her cold limbs or waning appetite, and hoped a few days of rest would calm things down. She knew she held things in to the detriment of her body but it had never gotten this severe before. She also knew if she opened up to Edra about how recent events had been affecting her, she would throw them both back into chaos, so she opted to keep her own counsel and ride out the physical distress while hoping for the best. "I am feeling better," she lied.

Edra, in desperation, had sent a note with Ben to Doc Nichols that said, *Mildred still looks pale. Can you come out please?*

Doc arrived early on the morning of the next day just as the women were finishing breakfast. Edra was relieved they were up and at the kitchen table, avoiding having to deal with the chance that Doc might ask to see Mildred in bed. She had been preoccupied with that one bed and Mildred's weakened condition.

"Morning, Mildred," he greeted her as he placed his black case down on the table.

Mildred looked at Edra with slight annoyance. "You sent for him?"

"Yes, she did," he said. "I was planning on coming anyway to see how you're getting on."

"I am feeling better…just needed the rest."

"Edra thinks you look pale. I tend to agree with her this time. Let me have a listen to your chest." He pulled the stethoscope out of his bag, put in the earpieces, and held the diaphragm over several areas above Mildred's heart. He then listened to her lungs. He took the tubes out of his ears. "Everything sounds okay. Your heart rate is slow and steady. Doesn't sound like an anemia. Lungs are clear. Let's have a look at your mouth. Open up. Edra, can you bring that lamp a little closer?"

Edra held up the nearest lamp for Doc to have a look.

"Tongue looks pink enough but your mouth is dry."

"What's that mean?" Edra asked, somewhat disquieted.

He looked at Edra. "She needs to drink more water. A little dehydration can make you tired." He turned back to face Mildred, "Keep taking what I gave you to build your iron. Looks like it's helping. But you need to keep at it with the water."

Edra gave Mildred a look that said, *I told you so.*

Doc put away his stethoscope. "I'll come back out in a few days. Meanwhile, send a note with Ben if you need me sooner." He started to leave then turned back. "I almost forgot. Mildred, Charley wanted to know if he could come see you?"

Mildred hesitated.

Edra jumped in, "Do you really think she's ready for company?"

"Well, okay then. I'll just let that be." Doc was about to turn to leave when Mildred looked like she wanted to say something.

Mildred felt guilty. After all, Charley had helped her return home from her spell in town and it didn't feel right to keep avoiding his requests to come visit. She was sure he didn't have a love interest in her but did not understand why he gave her so much attention. She pushed away the thoughts and focused back to Doc. "Well, maybe…"

"You want him to come?" asked Edra.

A nod followed Mildred's tentativeness. "Oh sure, go ahead and tell him to come on out tomorrow early afternoon."

"I think it'll do you some good to have company." Doc said his farewells and left.

Edra kept her frustration to herself.

*

The next day Charley stopped by Gus's to pick up some ground chocolate for Mildred. When he arrived at the Dunlap's ranch he found Mildred and Edra sitting on the porch bench reading. "Good to see you Mildred, Edra." He handed the bag to Mildred. "Thought you might like some hot chocolate. Had me some the other night and it was quite tasty."

"Thank you, Charley. That was nice of you," said Mildred.

Edra put down her book and took the bag from Mildred's hand. "I'll go and put on some water. We can all have some together." She was in better spirits than the day before since Mildred looked rosier in her cheeks and appeared to have more energy.

Charley sat on a chair across from Mildred. "You feeling better?"

There followed an awkward silence, then Mildred responded as if rehearsed. "Why yes, I am. What have you been doing to keep yourself busy?"

"Helping the children after school, doing some carpentry work, and had a couple of meals with Gus."

"Gus?" She was surprised since she knew Gus usually kept to himself.

"Never really know about someone till they start to open up. He's an interesting man, that Gus. Had some good food, good conversation, and I borrowed a book from him. I'm almost finished with it. I see you and Edra were reading. Do you like to read?"

"Yes. We both do. What book are you reading?" She was relieved the conversation shifted to a neutral subject, and not onto any talk of town gossip or happenings.

Edra interrupted them, carrying a tray with three cups of hot chocolate and a plate of oatmeal cookies that she had baked earlier that day. "Made these for your visit."

Charley reached out for a cup and picked up a cookie. "These sure do look good." He took a bite. "Darn good indeed."

Edra offered Mildred a cup, helped herself, put the tray down near Charley, and sat in a chair next to the bench, facing him.

Mildred turned to Edra, "Charley was telling me he borrowed a book from Gus. I was just about to find out what he's reading."

"*Uncle Tom's Cabin.* There was a page in the book that told about the author. Gus has all sorts of files on history, authors, all sorts of things."

"Interesting," replied Mildred.

"Yes. It is interesting what I learned about this book and the author…"

"Harriet Beecher Stowe," said Edra.

Mildred smiled.

"Yes. That's the name. Gus told me she was the first to put a Negro as a main character in a book."

Edra's interest perked. She commented, "There's rumor that President Lincoln met her and joked about her being the woman who wrote the book that started the Civil War."

Mildred added, "Next to the Bible, that book sold more copies than any other book."

The three of them continued their conversation for close to an hour with Charley and Edra doing most of the talking. Mildred watched and took it as a good sign that Edra indulged Charley in conversation, something new for her. *Perhaps he does just want some friends to visit with. Maybe Edra senses that.*

Finally, Edra noticed Mildred's attention waning. "Well Charley, if you'll excuse us, it's starting to get a little late."

"Thank you again for the hot chocolate," said Mildred.

"Well, I sure enjoyed our visit today. Would it be okay if I come again tomorrow?"

Edra stood, ignoring his request. "Let me walk you to your horse."

When out of earshot from Mildred, Edra commented, "Doc says she needs to rest. It's going to take a few days for the iron to work. I think it'd be best to hold off on another visit so soon." Charley nodded with understanding and mounted his horse.

Edra walked back through a trail of dust left by Charley's horse to find Mildred on the porch nodding off. She was proud of herself that she found the gumption to assist him to leave and curtailed any immediate future plans.

"Always forgive your enemies; nothing annoys them so much." OSCAR WILDE

18

Mail and packages from around the world arrive at Carson City by train. From there they are picked up by stagecoach and transported to outlying areas where tracks have not yet been laid. The twelve-hour trip, over a seventy-mile expanse, the safe limit for horses to travel in a day, ends up at the telegraph office in Red River Pass, which doubles for the post office.

Hanah Larue was in the telegraph office when Gus entered. Charley was also there installing a cabinet he had repaired for Satchel. "Hanah." He nodded. "Hey, Charley. Satchel."

Satchel gave Hanah her receipt and welcomed Gus. "You here for your package?"

"You bet." Gus replied.

Hanah fumbled with her purse, pretending to have difficulty placing her mail in it.

Satchel reached under the counter and pulled out a small package. "From Bonwit on Sixth Avenue. This looks like the one." He handed the package to Gus.

"That's it. Been waiting for these rings to come in."

Hanah dropped her purse to the floor, scattering the letters.

Just then Charley completed his work. "Okay, I'm done here."

Satchel hesitated. "Give me a minute here Gus, while I pay Charley…"

"We can settle up later. You're busy." Charley packed up his tools, made his way to the front of the counter, where he patted Gus on the back. "Rings there?" He smiled, then continued, joking, "That's gonna make someone happy." He walked out laughing.

Rings! Hanah thought as she tried to listen in and wondered if Josie had been right. Who else would order rings? There's no one. We'd have heard. She could not get out of there fast enough. She ran to Sarah's place and couldn't believe her luck when she found Josie there. "You were right!" She started to relay what had occurred.

"I told you!" said Josie.

Sarah in the kitchen heating up water yelled, "Wait for me." She approached carrying a tray with a pot of tea and three cups. "Here you are. Would you like me to pour…"

"Never mind that," said Josie. "Let her finish what she was saying."

"So, where was I?"

"Gus got the rings," prompted Josie.

"Rings?" Sarah blew on her tea.

Josie shot her a look to shut up.

Hanah continued and the story took on an unrecognizable twist.

"Charley thanked Gus for getting him a ring?" Sarah was dumbfounded. "You're kidding!"

"Well, it was something to that effect. Haven't seen Charley that happy in a long time. Left laughing. They come all the way from Sixth Avenue in New York City! Some fancy place."

Josie was ready to come out of her chair. "I told you! I knew it! Why, that vile woman!"

"I can't believe he's going to marry her," from Sarah. "I don't know about this."

Josie indignantly replied. "Oh, come on! You know something is going on with Charley and Mildred. She passed out. Now the ring arrives. Mildred hasn't been seen around. Put the pieces together."

"You do have a point," Sarah agreed.

Josie smiled peccantly. "I think we should pay the Dunlap's ranch a visit."

*

The cyclone in Josie's head had picked up speed as she thought and rethought what she heard. She'd been after Mildred for years, to no avail. Now she had her chance and knew this was something that wouldn't just run off Mildred's back like the sweat pouring down hers. If it were the last thing she ever did, she was determined to bring Mildred down. Later that day, she had tea at the cafe with Annalee, who commented that Helene must know something. "Why, that Helene. I'll have her neck for not saying anything to me. I knew the minute I saw them at the lake that something was going on. Didn't I tell you?"

Pat walked up to the table, "Did I just hear you talking about Mildred and Charley? Biggest surprise this town's seen, the two of them! Did I really hear you say engaged?"

Josie left the café and went to collect her children from the schoolhouse, where she ran into Charley. "Finished with the kids today?"

"Yeah," he replied.

With hackles raised, a feigned smile, and as much pleasantry as she could bring herself to display to elicit a response in him, she said, "I'm happy for you, Charley."

Unsuspecting anything devious, he assumed that she was referring to his borrowing books and spending time with Gus. "Yeah, never thought it'd turn out to be so much fun. Gus's really been helpful."

*

The next day Josie, bent on finding out what Helene knew, amassed Annalee, Sarah and Madeline. Hanah, home with an ill child, was not along. They made their way through the vast expanse of dust and watched the covered variety of plants-turned-tumbleweed bounce about in the wake of their motion. A few wisps of clouds moved along with them in the enervating heat as they rode out to the Whitmore's place. When they arrived they ran into Frank, wiping sweat from his face with a handkerchief. "Ladies," Frank greeted them on his way to the house from the barn, "what brings you all out here today?"

126

"Is Helene home?" asked Josie.

"Inside. Go ahead on in. Be a little quiet. The baby's sleeping."

Annalee could not contain herself. "Of all things, Frank. Probably make life easier for you now."

"Come again?"

Annalee blurted, "Charley and Mildred."

"Charley and Mildred what?"

"Why, their engagement."

Josie nudged Annalee's foot in an attempt to stop her from saying anything else.

Frank nearly fell over. "What the hell are you talking about!"

Helene ran out. "What's the yelling? The boy's asleep." She was surprised to see the women.

Frank started to seethe. "Helene, what do you know about this?"

"About what?"

Josie laughed under her breath, delighted she had stirred the pot, a sweet consequence of meddling. She was determined to get everyone riled up then blame it all on Mildred for getting Charley involved with her. Emotions running high at her causation empowered her and she was delighted she had succeeded at drawing others in.

"Annalee, would you care to repeat what you just told me?" commanded Frank.

Annalee, now embarrassed, said, "You haven't heard? Why, Josie told me…"

Josie snapped back. "I didn't tell you nothing. Hanah was the one who heard it. Right from the horse's mouth. You were there with me, Sarah. You heard her."

Frank, exasperated, asked, "And what did Hanah hear from whom?"

Sarah answered him. "Charley got a ring for Mildred."

A startled Helene stepped back. "A ring? What…"

"Seems your friends are telling us that Charley and Mildred are engaged."

Helene was astonished. "What?"

"You haven't heard yet?" Josie pointed her question to Helene. But before giving her a chance to answer, she continued. "Maybe they were just too wrapped up in each other to come around here and tell you," Josie said to Frank with edged sarcasm.

Frank turned red in the face. "That's enough out of you. All of you. Helene, if you've got anything to do with this…" he fumed.

"This is the first I've heard," Helene pleaded.

Frank yelled, "Out of here! All of you! We've got work to do!"

As he watched the women leave, he hissed to Helene, "If you had anything to do this with, I swear to you…"

She tried to defend herself against Frank's anger. "I'm telling you the truth. This is the first I've heard."

"Bunch of nonsense. My sister's husband engaged to Mildred!"

"Frank, your sister is gone…"

"Shut up! You shut your mouth. Not a word about Emma. There's no way…"

She cowered. "What if it's true? What if they just hadn't told us yet?"

"I told you to shut up! You listen to me and keep that mouth of yours out of this. If I find out you had anything to do with this…" Frank was so enraged that it was all he could do but turn around and go back to the barn.

Helene, still surging with anxious energy, went inside, looked in on little Frankie sleeping through the commotion, and made some sage brew. It took her several minutes to become calm from Frank's upset.

*

An unsuspecting Mildred woke up feeling refreshed, the best she'd felt since all the dealings began with Charley. She attributed this to the fact that Edra had relaxed about their situation since his visit. She was pleased that he came to talk about the books he was reading, since she knew how much Edra loved to read and talk about stories she became involved in. Again, she had also had enough time away from the over-stimulation to relax emotionally and physically.

"You are looking better," Edra commented.

"Yeah, I feel back to my old self."

"That's a relief, Mil."

"Think it's time I go back to town." Mildred told Edra she felt that her recent physical problems were all but resolved and she felt strong. Edra could see the validity of that in her demeanor and complexion and did not resist. Mildred got ready, hitched Lil to the buggy, then headed to town. She arrived at Gus's before the usual flood of customers, took care of shopping business, and then made her way to Charley's to surprise him. He had just returned from helping the children at school.

"Mildred. Good to see you here. You feeling better?" He was pleasantly surprised.

"Yes. A little rest and I'm back as good as new," she smiled.

"It's early but how's about we grab a bite to eat?"

"That'd be fine."

"Let me just wash up and get ready. Would you like to walk over to Barney's?"

Mildred remembered the last time they were there. The idea of running into Pat made her cringe but she knew that she would have to face her again at some point. "Sure, be good to stretch my legs."

After Charley cleaned up, they walked up his street, turned down Main Street, and made their way to the cafe. Satchel and Jake Cummings, standing in front of the telegraph office, stopped talking as they approached. Charley nodded and continued on. Mildred was relieved she did not have to make any small talk. When they arrived at Barney's, and she noticed Pat was serving, her stomach seized up.

Pat caught sight of them and approached smiling. "Why, look whose here? Let's see…" She looked around. "Yes, I've got a table for you over there." She pointed to a table in the middle of the room and escorted them over to it. That was the last place Mildred wanted to sit and Pat's uncharacteristic friendliness gave her a bad feeling in the pit of her stomach. Before she had a chance to sit, Pat blurted out in a loud voice, "I understand congratulations are due."

A hush settled over the other customers in the cafe. All eyes turned toward Charley and Mildred.

"Congratulations over what?" asked Charley as he helped Mildred to her seat and took his.

Mildred felt a sinking feeling.

"Why Charley! You'd keep us all guessing till you two went and got married."

"What!" Charley in a reflex motion pushed back his chair. "What in heaven's name…"

"And Mildred, this is nice news for you. Lunch's on the house. I'll be right back." Grinning, Pat left them to get the menu.

The color drained from Mildred's face. "What is this about?" she whispered to Charley.

"I have no idea."

She felt trapped with all eyes on them and all she could entertain was he had lied to her and was somehow in on this. *How could I have been so stupid? So blind to walk into this?* She didn't have the time to think this through and see that this was what she fundamentally wanted, which was for him to reject her. She was too taken aback by the surprise, the jolt, that she had been so wrong about him. *But why should he be any different than anyone else? The whole damn town's been making fun of me for years!*

She was accustomed to being talked about, ridiculed behind her back, but this forthright public display and embarrassment made her livid.

"Mildred, I didn't know…"

"Not here." She worked to maintain her composure.

They ordered and Mildred forced herself to eat a sandwich.

At a distance, Pat snickered to herself, "Oh, this is good."

Charley saw it, and wanted to get up and slap her. He felt helpless to do anything but sit there and be civil.

Mildred took his lack of action as reinforcement that she was right about him, that he was out to humiliate her.

Charley, still dumbfounded, motioned for the check. He paid it and they left without speaking. The silence continued on the walk back to Charley's, where he saw Lil nervously pacing and knew her horse sensed that something was wrong. He was still confounded by Pat's outburst and didn't know what to say. He didn't know how to rectify something when he had no idea what brought it on and saw Mildred shutting down, burning up inside. His way was to meet confrontation with silence until he had a grasp on what was happening, and then he would try to address it, but here he was at a loss for anything to say other than to repeat, "I had no idea…"

"That'll be enough, Charley." She stepped into her buggy, hit her whip to Lil, and screamed, "Go!"

Mildred fumed the entire ride back. Midway, she let out a yell where she was sure no one would hear. "God damn it all to hell! I hate this town!" She swung the driving whip over Lil. "Move girl! Move!" Lil's trot picked up to a gallop and the horse moved with unbridled spirit, leaving clouds of sand right up to Mildred's front door.

She stormed in, slamming the door so hard that the dining room table shook and a lamp fell over. She picked up the first object she set eyes on, a glass vase, and threw it up against the wall, waking Edra who was napping in the bedroom.

"I've had it!" Mildred screamed. "I'm finished with this town!" She picked up one of her mother's antique bowls and smashed it onto the floor.

Edra entered the living room dazed. "Mildred?"

"Start packing! We're leaving this place. I've had just about all I'm going to take!"

"What?"

"God damn those small-minded meddling…they have no life so they have to get into everybody else's!"

"You're scaring me." Edra put a hand on Mildred's back. "Calm down. Tell me what happened."

Mildred pulled away, stomping and ranting. "Get the suitcases out!"

"Please," Edra begged as tears welled in her eyes.

"You were right to question the dumb plan! The damn bigots won't let us live in peace! And as for Charley…he's just trying to embarrass me. Have another laugh on Mildred! God damn them all!"

Edra's attempts and pleads for Mildred to calm down and tell her what happened fell on deaf ears. What had been pent up inside Mildred for years; all the abuse and ridicule she had taken from people who did not know her and had judged her harshly; the suppression of her emotional reactions to the vindictiveness she had personally incurred; the years of putting on a false front, and smiling in the face of persecution exploded out of her. Worse was she felt utter helplessness over the lack of control she felt in protecting the one good thing in her life, her relationship with Edra.

Edra knew there was nothing to do but allow it. She stayed by Mildred till she started to quiet then asked, "Can we talk now?"

Mildred told her what happened. "All he said was he had no idea. No idea, my foot! Oh, everyone in there got a good eyeful…"

"Mil, I'm so sorry you had to experience this. But what if he is interested? I told you he might be. He was so nice here the other day."

"He sat there and did nothing! This isn't the action of someone interested in me! I nearly choked on what I was eating! He's like all the rest of them."

"Is there any way there's a misunderstanding here? You thought he seemed genuine when he helped you at Doc's. You're usually a good judge of character."

Mildred was despondent. "I'm not a good judge of anything."

"Mil, let's just sit tight on this for now," said Edra. "I'll make us some chamomile tea."

Mildred had wanted Charley to reject her romantic reaches but what she never considered was he would go out of his way to make a complete fool of her. This was harder for her to take than the planned rejection by him. They had a cup of tea, talked more calmly, and decided they would sleep on it and determine in a new light how they wanted to handle the situation.

*

Charley slept fitfully, unable to keep his mind from going over what had happened. He was sure he knew who started it all and that it was designed to embarrass Mildred. She had been a victim of mockery for years and he was fed up with all the nonsense.

The next morning he rode out to his brother-in-law's place, fit to be tied.

"Helene!" he yelled through the open door as he let himself in.

"Quiet, Charley. The baby…"

"Outside!" Charley demanded as he motioned to the front door.

Helene followed him nervously, hoping that Frank would remain down at the barn out of earshot.

"Did you start that rumor about me and Mildred being engaged?"

"Rumor?" It was the only word that caught her attention. She had hoped it was true.

"It was you! Wasn't it?"

"What?"

"You heard me!"

"This is the first I heard any such thing," she lied.

"Oh, come on now. What do you take me for? I'm not the dumb moron you all think I am. You've been niggling away at me to get with Mildred right from the get go. Your meddling has gone too far. You hang around with those women, the likes of Josie…"

"I had nothing…"

"Mildred's done nothing but help your family out. Your no-good gossiping is just hurting good people, but no, you don't care a lick about that. Not a decent bone in any of you."

A very nervous Helene responded. "You have to believe me. I had nothing to do with this. I'll go talk to Mildred."

"You'll do nothing of the sort. You stay away from her! And stay out of my business!"

Just then, Frank walked up with Mabel. "Hey, Charley! Our cow just popped. Want to see the calf?"

"Baby cow!" Mabel ran to hug Charley. "Come see. Come see."

"Hiya honey," he said to the child, as he swallowed his anger. "I have some work I need to be getting back to." He gave Mabel a warm hug, avoided Helene, and reached out a hand to Frank. "Maybe next time."

A very jittery Helene stepped back out of his way, relieved Frank made no mention about the earlier visit from the ladies.

"Yeah, we had some rough times with her," said Frank as they shook hands.

"Sorry I don't have more time to stay." Charley turned and rode away in a hurry, leaving the others standing there.

"Arguments are to be avoided: They are always vulgar and often convincing." OSCAR WILDE

19

As Gus swept the porch of his shop, Josie and Pat arrived, yapping about what happened at the cafe. He overheard Pat saying, "They came into the cafe yesterday. I congratulated them. Shut the whole place up. What a scene. Don't think they said two words to each other." She stopped to greet Gus.

He responded with a slight nod, "Pat, Josie," and then escaped into the store to leave the two women to their chatter.

Within a few minutes, they followed Gus in. Pat picked up a basket and headed down the grain aisle while Josie headed to the counter. "Little under the weather today, Gus. Do you have any lozenges?"

"Sure thing." He went to the aisle where elixirs were displayed, got a pack of lozenges and returned. "Here you go." She had a peculiar look on her face that made him feel uneasy.

"So tell me, Gus. Which ring did Charley pick out?" asked Josie.

"What?"

"Their engagement. Word's all over town."

Gus was flabbergasted. "Where in heaven's name did you get that idea?"

"From Charley, who else?"

"Charley Milpass told you he's engaged to Mildred? He came out and told you that?"

"Well, not in those exact words."

"And?"

"I saw him when I dropped the kids off. Congratulated him. He didn't deny it. Then Hanah was in the telegraph office when you got the rings. Who else…"

"Are you kidding me? You congratulated Charley for being engaged?"

"Well, Helene also told me they were seeing a lot of each other."

"Did she tell you they were engaged?"

"Not exactly," said Josie.

Pat approached to pay for her items.

Josie asked, "How come you got a whole order of rings in?"

Gus was way too annoyed to be civil. "Not that it's any of your business, but that shipment was for Zack Langford's General Store over at Walker Junction. To cut shipping expenses we order together." He shook his head in disgust over what he imagined was spreading through town at the expense of Mildred and Charley. He was usually good about keeping his composure but this, in addition to all the trouble Josie and her brood had caused by their irresponsible babble, pushed the envelope for him.

Pat gave Josie a dirty look.

"There's still other things going on with them. Probably should be engaged," responded Josie defiantly.

"And what in the hell do you mean by that?" Gus knew he had better cool down before he really lost it. "Oh never mind. What's the use in trying to put any sense in your heads."

Pat and Josie silently paid for their purchases and left the store.

✳

Charley was in an unhappy state. He did not want to go out to see Mildred without letting her have some cooling down time. He also did not want to go home and be alone. He rode out in the desert and found a quiet place to sit upon a mound of rocks among a few scattered sagebrush plants. In the dead heat, his head buzzed with anger and sorrow bouncing back and forth, riveting around like bullets striking hard ideas that gave no relief. He was about to move when he heard a hiss and looked to the direction it was coming from. A movement of brush, too close to his legs to make a run for, prompted him to reach back to his horse and grab his rifle. He readied it in the direction where the movement increased. *Thanks for warning me you're there.* The rattler slithered out into view. With the barrel pointed and finger on the trigger, he waited as it wound closer, now less than a foot away, with its rattle sounding like dried bones grinding together indicating a warning before it strikes. *Man, you are one huge fellow!* He estimated it at least six feet long. He knew it had poor eyesight, would react to the vibration of movement, so he sat still, sweat dripping down his face, hoping that the one, maybe two, second window of danger would pass and the snake would change its mind and move away. The second he felt his horse get antsy, his finger hit the trigger, and time was up. No sooner was the rattler limp than a turkey vulture flew overhead, and another, until four were circling. He left nature to do what it does and rode back to town.

Still not wanting to be alone, he headed to Gus's, who was closing as he arrived. "Mind if I come in for a while, Gus?"

He took one look at Charley and knew what must be on his mind. "Come on in. I think we could both use a drink."

Charley nodded and followed Gus up the stairs.

"Want any food?" He handed Charley a shot glass of whiskey.

"Nah, thanks though. I'm not hungry."

Gus felt for Charley's misfortune, the undeserved injustice. He also sympathized for Mildred's plight. It was not lost on him that they were both good people. She was helpful to most of the people in town when financial need arose and kept to herself, minding her own business, and maintaining her manners in the face of challenging adversity. He also knew Charley to be a kind man, who tended to his wife during the worst of their time together, helped the kids at school, did odd carpenter jobs for people who couldn't afford to pay him, and also steered clear of gossip. Of all the people in town, Charley and Mildred were among the handful of decent people who did not deserve the hand they were dealt. "I had words with Josie today. Heard what must be bothering you."

"Where's all this coming from, Gus? What the hell is wrong with people? Josie's too damned bored. She has to get into everybody else's business. She's the worst of them."

"It's not boredom with Josie. I kinda feel sorry for her."

"What! Feel sorry for her? Are you kidding me? What's to feel sorry for! Why, I'd like to slap some sense into her and all the rest of those meddling busybodies." Charley held his glass out for another pour.

"She can't help her hatred."

"Oh come on, Gus!"

"I'm not just making conversation here. I know some things about her."

"Like what?" Charley, filled with disgust, continued, "There's nothing…" He gulped down what was in his glass and banged it on the table indicating he wanted another. "There's just no excuse."

"Oh, I agree with you there. All I'm saying is there's a reason. You learn about someone and it changes things."

The booze was softening his brain. Half-facetiously he asked, "So what's this big sob story?"

He took a long look at Charley, the new wrinkles formed around his bloodshot eyes, the stubble of beard, all signs of the strain he was under. "I really don't like meddling or telling other's business. There's enough of that going around." Although he was reluctant to continue, he knew it was the right thing to do to help his friend understand. "I trust you, Charley, or I wouldn't say a thing. If you knew a few things it might help take some of the sting out. Help you understand."

"Understand whaaaa?"

"Josie has some history." Gus went on to relay that when Josie's mamma took ill she had to sell whatever she could to make ends meet. She sold him a box of books that she'd kept since she was much younger. It was the last of the worldly possessions that meant anything to her. She told him there were antique books and possessions that were too painful for her to look at before giving them away. Without appraising the content, he made her a charitable offer and watched her cry as she left the box behind. When he opened it and went through the items, he found a journal. On the inside cover was inscribed this diary belongs to Mary Calhoun, Josie's mother.

Charley made a face that he could care less.

"I see you're disgusted. I would be too. I don't need to continue if you'd rather I didn't."

Not wanting to take out his anger on Gus, and still alert enough to follow the conversation, he relented. "Go on."

"Josie's mamma must have forgot she put it there. I knew she didn't want to look at the things she left and I didn't want to intrude in her privacy, so I put it in a drawer and there it sat for several weeks, until…I'm a little embarrassed to admit, my curiosity got to me." He went on to explain that their family lived in the south, Georgia to be exact. Last name was Calhoun. Before the Civil War broke out, they owned a small cotton plantation and a few slaves. When Sherman came through, he burned it to the ground after he seized their cotton crop and freed their slaves. Left them destitute. Their rich relatives refused to lift a finger to help them.

"Who were they related to?" asked Charley.

"Calhoun doesn't ring a bell? They were distant relatives of John C. Calhoun who had been Vice-President of the United States. James Calhoun, mayor of Atlanta during the war, was also a relative. Josie was just a toddler at the time."

"That still dun 'splain why she did what she did. I don't care what her story is. Don't make it right!" He downed another shot.

"No it doesn't. There's more."

"I don't really give a damn 'bout Josie." Charley, numb of any emotion, his brain swelling in liquor, held up his glass. "But for you, old Gus, I'll lissen."

Gus obligingly poured. "After the war, when the Carpetbaggers came to the South and took over reconstruction, Josie's father left Georgia and took his family to Virginia City to seek his fortune in the mines of the Comstock Lode. He never succeeded and died in a mine accident. Her mother took in laundry to feed the children."

Charley swatted at a fly buzzing around his face.

"Josie had two older brothers."

That cut through the inebriation, sending an alert adrenaline rush through Charley, getting his attention. "I thought she had no family outside Satchel and their kids."

"That's true. Her brothers both died of pneumonia. Was during that cold winter spell we had in these parts many years ago. Lot of folk perished back then. That's about it."

"That still don't excuse her vindictiveness to Mildred. She's plain got it in for that woman for no good reason."

Gus solemnly replied, "You haven't made the connection because you probably don't know that Max Dunlap was from Ohio. Came out here and bought up every piece of land he could. Took over."

"So?"

"Sherman was from Ohio. Sherman's march to the sea…"

It took Charley a moment then it hit him. "You think Josie's family had it in for Mildred's father because of Sherman? That's really a far stretch even for you, Gus. I don't buy it at all."

"From what Josie's mom wrote, Max and Sherman could have been brothers." Gus went on to explain that they were both tall, over six feet, had reddish hair, and thin statures. Josie's mom wrote about Sherman being orphaned when he was nine, then getting lucky by being adopted by a wealthy family who put him into the best schools. *He was handed so much, then goes on in his life to destroy others? He destroyed us. Just like Max Dunlap did when he bought up all that land. Took every last parcel. Left nothing for anyone else around here! Men like you don't deserve what you got! Men like you don't deserve to live! Damn you, Sherman. Damn you, Max Dunlap!* Gus went on to say that Josie's mom had the two confused in her mind and was bent on getting even with Sherman through her vengeance for Max. What tipped the scales for her was all the land Max owned, from the Preemption Act, at what she felt was the expense of her family. There were no homesteading parcels left after Max manipulated all the land for himself. She blamed Max, just like she blamed Sherman for taking away their land. The only hope her family had was to get in on the free land deals, but they were too late because of Dunlap.

"What's that got to do with Josie's way with Mildred?" asked Charley.

"Josie's mom hated anything associated with the Dunlap name, including Mildred. She passed her hatred along to Josie. It's obvious Josie hates all that Mildred's inherited." He took a handkerchief out of his pocket and wiped the beads of sweat from his face. "There was also the similarity of physical appearance…"

"What?"

"I don't want to be saying anything unkind about Mildred," Gus replied. He did not want to say that Mildred was tall and masculine-looking like Max.

"Then don't! It still doesn't satisfy me as to why she has it in for Mildred."

"Who can explain the hatred we learn from our parents? Why we believe what we do? It runs deep and is very complicated. You haven't been exposed to it like I have so I understand why you find this so diffi-cult to understand or accept. Even without Josie's mamma's feelings about Max or any Dunlap, she could have developed her hatred just because Mildred is powerful and represents everything Josie lost: land, power, even her inheritance. All that hatred bundled up and directed at one woman, Mildred."

"That little bitch!"

"Yes, there is that side of Josie. But there's also all this other stuff buried in her."

Charley felt wiped out and withdrawn from everything Gus had said. "All the persecution of Mildred through the years, escalated because of Josie. I don't know why Mildred puts up with it. Shows me she's a good woman."

"It is a very sad thing that nowadays there is so little useless information." OSCAR WILDE

20

As the effect of the alcohol wore off during the night, Charley's addled mind played the conversation with Gus over and over until he saw what Gus was tying to tell him without his reaction clouding it. Although he didn't accept the excuse of Josie's childhood as a reason to hate someone she hardly knew, he now understood that she was haunted by her past. It didn't change how he felt about her, but what he hoped for was this would give him the opportunity he needed to mend things with Mildred. After three days of no response from her to his notes, a very tired and agitated Charley grew too impatient to wait any longer and decided to pay her an unannounced visit.

"Hello? Anybody here?" he called through the front door. "Mildred, you home?"

There was no reply.

"Edra?"

Yet no reply.

He waited. "Someone!"

After five minutes of calling and knocking, he gingerly let himself in.

He walked through the living room to a hallway at the back of the house where he saw two closed doors. Without thinking, he went to the door on the left and opened it to find an empty den full of what looked like office furniture. He then went to the other door and on impulse turned the knob and pushed it ajar, enough to see Mildred asleep in the bed. She stirred but did not wake. He closed the door.

Just then, Edra walked into the house carrying a bunch of freshly cut flowers from the garden. The minute she saw the backside of Charley at her bedroom door, she dropped the flowers and screamed, "What are you doing there?" She was relieved to see the door shut.

He quickly turned around. "I need to talk to Mildred."

"Get out!"

Mildred woke up. "Edra, what's…"

Edra ran up to Charley and pulled him away from the bedroom door. "Leave! Right now!"

"I need to talk to her. It's really…"

"She doesn't want to see you! Now go!"

Mildred overheard the commotion and in a panic put on a robe, opened the door, and rushed into the living room. "What! Edra, did you let him in?"

"I let myself in."

"Get out!" Edra screamed.

"Please, just hear me out. Then I'll…"

"Now! I'm going to get the shotgun if you don't leave!" screamed Edra.

"Please, listen to me," he begged.

Edra ran to the den and fumbled with the gun cabinet latch that refused to open. "Damn it!"

"Charley, you need to leave." Mildred was adamant. She felt herself drain of the little energy she gained from yet another fitful night's sleep.

"If you'll just listen to me, I can explain."

Edra stormed back to the living room. "Get out of here!"

Mildred reached for a chair to steady herself. "Please, just go," she panted.

He made a move toward her. "Let me help you."

Edra jumped between them. "You've done enough! Now, go."

"I haven't done anything. That's what I'm trying to tell you."

Mildred was sweating profusely, her rheumy eyes out of focus, fatigue dulling her response time. "Please, Charley, I'm too tired to argue."

Edra helped Mildred to sit. She shot Charley a look. "For the love of mercy, will you please just go."

It pained him to see Mildred so weak and ashen. For a moment, he wanted to turn around and leave but caught himself. He knew if he walked out now he wouldn't have another opportunity to get through to them, and he felt that what he had to say would help. "Let me just have my say and I'll leave. Please."

When Mildred saw how crestfallen he was, she stopped resisting. She nodded to Edra it was okay. "Go on then."

"I had dinner with Gus a couple nights ago." He told them about what Gus had relayed to him about the rings and how the rumor most likely got started.

"Why didn't you say anything to Pat? You just sat there letting her believe…"

"A lie. I know. I feel real bad about that."

"Why?" Mildred repeated.

"It was so awkward. Everyone was looking at us. Truth is, I didn't know what to say. Didn't want to draw any more attention. I was afraid it'd get worse for you."

"But you didn't say anything."

"I tried to and you stopped me, a couple of times."

Mildred saw he was right, that he did try to mention he didn't know, but she was too taken aback by the whole situation when she cut him off.

Edra wanted to be sure she understood what he said. "You're saying you had absolutely nothing to do with this?"

"That's right."

"Then how'd this get started? No one questioned you? And we know no one talked to Mildred."

He spoke gingerly. "My guess is, Josie. I know it may sound

THE PERSECUTION OF MILDRED DUNLAP

outlandish but I really think…"

Mildred sucked in a breath. "It's not a surprise to me."

"I'm sorry for all of this, Mildred. That you have to put up with her misguided vengeance."

When Mildred asked him what he meant by that, he explained further what he had learned from Gus. He knew it was the right thing to let them in. As he talked, Mildred appreciated his sincerity and when he was finished she labored to get a breath in. "I'm tired. Think it'd be good if you left now," without any further mention of Josie.

An apprehensive Edra sat still.

"Sure hope I didn't tire you out too much. I just had to be sure we're okay."

"I'm fine with you. Don't know what to do about the rest of the town. We need to think this through"

Charley responded, "Okay. I was thinking…"

"I meant me and Edra." Mildred knew they would probably do nothing. Let the pieces fall where they may and distance herself from Charley, which he would understand. The embarrassment in town could work to their advantage.

"Oh sure. Sorry. However, I think it's high time I have a word with Josie."

"I wouldn't do that." Mildred was brusque, which all but drained the last of her energy.

"She needs to be stopped. All of them with their mouths."

Edra interrupted, "Then what? They've caused enough trouble." She saw Mildred's effort to breathe. "Give us some time to figure out what we want to do."

"Okay, but I don't understand…"

Edra jumped on him. "Charley! You do want to help, don't you?"

"Why yes, but…"

"Then we're asking you to just let it be. We've had enough excitement today."

"Sure, well would it be okay if I come back out again soon?"

"Let's just let it be for now." Edra walked him to the door, watched

145

him leave, then turned to Mildred. "I had no idea it was that bad with Josie."

"Now you understand what I've been telling you about her. Why we need to protect ourselves. All this time I thought her animosity against me was cause we didn't go to church. This takes the cake!"

"Mil, I'm worried about you. You look so pasty. I thought you were going to faint when Charley was here."

"We'll be okay," she mumbled back. "It's working out okay. We can turn this to our advantage." She slumped down in the chair. "I just need a little more rest to get my strength back."

Edra knew it was Mildred's pattern to hold things in. She hoped she was right about things turning around. She also hoped the turbulence wasn't taking a toll on Mildred's body.

*

Charley rode back to his place feeling relief they heard him out, but he was not happy with how Mildred looked and that he had agreed to say nothing to Josie. That wasn't the only thing that bothered him about the visit; something else stuck in his craw. *How come you only have one bed?* He went back over the scene in his mind, trying to remember if he missed something. There was the den with a desk, couple of chairs, a cabinet where the guns were kept, another cabinet containing miscellaneous items, but no bed in that room, and he was sure he only saw one in the other room. It was the one Mildred was sleeping in. *Maybe Edra sleeps on the couch?* He wanted to come up with some other answer than what was niggling at him, but deep down he knew what he saw, not just in their bedroom but how they interacted with each other. He remembered the inflection in Mildred's voice when she first spoke of Edra to him, how they tended to each other, and showed affection that was reminiscent of something all too familiar that he shared with Emma. A chill ran down his spine when he thought of Mildred's subtle masculine mannerisms. He was a slave to the thoughts that refused to cease. The one thing that puzzled him was why Mildred was showing an interest in him.

When a week passed, he sent a note with Ben. Mildred responded she needed to rest. By the next week, the notes had stopped, while his overactive mind kept going. He tried to keep himself busy doing odd jobs and helping the kids after school. He borrowed books from Gus and read to fill the empty space. He said nothing to Josie or any of the other women, and made no trips out to his brother-in-law's place, and no one in town made any further comments to him about being engaged to Mildred. But the talk among the women continued.

"So what if they aren't engaged. My bet is he knocked her up," Josie snickered.

Madeline replied, "Where is Mildred, anyway?"

Josie laughed. "She's hiding her growing belly."

"What's Helene have to say about that?" asked Sarah.

Josie replied, "She's still waiting for Frank to cool off from our visit. We'll give them a little more time, and then head back out there. He'll have forgotten about it by then, and we can go check up on Mildred."

"Patriotism is the virtue of the vicious." OSCAR WILDE

21

Satchel Purdue heard the last of the news clickety-clack over the telegraph machine, when Sam Tucker entered.

"Got a telegram to send," said Sam.

"Give me just a couple minutes to finish this up here." Satchel finished what he was writing. "Cleveland is supporting his boy Olney, showing what we're all about!"

"President Cleveland?" asked Sam.

"Yes," Satchel replied, raising his eyebrows. "And listen here. It says Cleveland will address Congress about Olney's adopting a broad interpretation of the Monroe Doctrine, referencing a note sent to Britain demanding it submit…"

Sam asked, "Who's Olney?"

"Secretary of State. Olney says the U.S. has authority to mediate border disputes in the Western Hemisphere. He demanded Britain submit a dispute to arbitration!"

"Can you translate that?" laughed Sam.

"Venezuela requested support in its border dispute with Britain over the boundary between it and British Guiana. Cleveland will reinforce Olney's demand." Satchel paused in his amazement to read what he had just read to himself. "I couldn't be prouder of being an American today!"

Sam, still confused, asked, "What am I missing here?"

"Olney's demand reasserts United States sovereignty in the Western Hemisphere in accordance with the Monroe Doctrine. In simple terms, we're in charge and no one's gonna be messing with us! Hands off of us, Britain!"

Sam rejoiced. "Show them who has the gumption!"

"Sam, can I get you to drop this off at Gus's?"

"Sure thing, Satchel."

After Gus had posted the telegram, a crowd gathered around his noticeboard, the men cheering, shaking hands and patting each other on the back, the women giggling.

"What's all the commotion about?" asked Sheriff Roper as he entered the store to pick up a tin of tobacco.

"We got ourselves one powerful country here," Sam explained, pointing to the telegram that Gus had just posted.

Gus watched, thinking, *Yeah, and what's it going to cost us in lives? Goddamn hubris. When we ever gonna learn? Who's gonna be the next victim all this hostility will be unleashed on? There's no talking to this lot.* He was frustrated by the ignorance he saw all around him, the lack of compassion and understanding, even worse the complete poverty of any comprehension that a poison lived inside these individuals and as long as they kept pointing fingers and saw their hatred outside of themselves, nothing would come but destruction.

*

Another week passed and Charley still had not received a note from Mildred. Since he did not hear from Ben, he checked in with Doc daily to see if he had any word from the Dunlap's ranch, and became concerned when he heard that Edra had written that she wanted Doc to pay them a visit. He felt bad that his befriending Mildred had caused her so much turmoil and was taking a toll on her health. He wanted to send a message with Doc but opted out of that idea, feeling that patience, not adding more pressure, was best.

*

Doc had one last patient to see before he headed out to the Dunlap's ranch. Young Frankie Whitmore had been vomiting for nine hours, causing his little body to become listless. Helene, an anxious wreck since the ladies' visit, blamed herself for the baby's illness, sure it was her nerves upsetting his gut.

"He was active just two days ago," said Frank. "His eyes are so dark and sunken. Last three hours he barely moved."

"If he can't keep fluids in him, we're going to have to get him to Carson City." Nichols continued, "Get a sheet."

Helene went pale. "It can't be that bad? You'll be able to fix him, won't you Doc," she pleaded.

"Helene! Did you hear the Doc? Get a sheet."

She backed away to get it. "Here it is." Her hand was shaking. "He'll be okay, now that Doc's here. You're gonna fix our boy. I just know everything's gonna be…"

"Will you stop your yapping, woman, and let him do his work."

Doc wrapped the baby's arms in the sheet to hold him steady. He motioned for Frank to hold him bent with his buttocks out so he could administer medicine through the clyster.

"That'll hurt him!" Helene yelped.

Doc continued on with what he was doing. "That'll help with the vomiting. Frank, hold that leg still."

The baby gave a weak cry when Doc inserted the tiny tube. "That's not a good sign. He's too dehydrated to complain."

Helene's forehead drew beads of sweat.

When the medicine was inserted, Doc showed Frank how to hold the baby. Then to Helene, "If we can keep that in him, he should be able to take fluids orally." Fifteen minutes later Doc said, "Helene, go ahead and give him a bottle." Little Frankie's crying turned into screaming. "That's much better. He's getting more energy."

"Fine for you to say, Doc," Frank laughed. "He ain't screaming in your ears."

When she was finished giving her son his bottle, Helene commented, "His skin don't feel doughy anymore. That's a good thing, isn't it?"

"Yes," replied Doc.

"Don't know what I'd do if anything happened to my little guy," she whimpered.

Just then Mabel entered the living room door from outside. "Cranky had three balls in his mouth!"

"Shhhhhh honey. Doc's helping your brother here."

"What's wrong with him?" she squealed.

"We'll tell you later. Go and play in the bedroom," said Helene.

"I don't want to play alone anymore!"

Frank piped up, "Do what your mother says!"

Mabel retreated to the bedroom pouting.

Frank took a look at little Frankie and felt encouraged. "He's turning pink, Doc."

Comforted, Helene said, "Thank goodness. That's my good boy."

They waited for twenty minutes to see if the baby would vomit, and when he did not, Doc said to Frank out of earshot of Helene, "He'll be fine. Off now for my last patient."

"Who else you seeing this far out?" asked Frank.

"Your landlady."

"Give her our best," he said. "She's a good woman helping us so much."

"I'll be sure to pass that along." Doc packed up his things, gave Helen's shoulder a reassuring pat, shook hands with Frank, then said, "I'll be back out tomorrow to see how he's doing." He left and headed out to Mildred's place. When he arrived, Edra met him at the door. He could see that she had been crying.

"Sorry I'm so late. Been over at the Whitmore's. Had to get some fluids in their little one. How's Mildred doing?"

"She doesn't want to eat and only takes little bites to appease me. She's up at night tossing and turning. We can't keep up with the laundry from all the sweating. Her spirit is down. I'm worried about her." Although Mildred tried to reassure Edra things would turn to their benefit from the aftermath of what happened, it did nothing to assuage her worry.

"She's in the bedroom?"

"Yes, she's asleep now."

"If she hasn't been sleeping well, let's not disturb her right now. Let me talk to you first. How's about a cup of tea?"

Edra brought a tray with tea and biscuits to the living room and placed it on the side table.

"Thanks Edra. So tell me what's been happening with Mildred since I last saw her."

"She perked up. Seems the iron worked, but then she went to town."

"I heard about that."

Edra began crying. "It's just too much for anyone to deal with."

"Don't let it get to you. Everyone's attention is on the latest telegram. No one has their mind on Mildred and Charley."

"I wish that were true," mumbled Edra.

"Of course it's true. I'll tell ya, if I let everything that was said about me bother me, I'd take to my bed also," he laughed. "Then I'd high-tail it out of town."

He tried to play down the symptoms, to calm Edra. He'd been through this with them before. He knew Mildred held things in tightly. Through the years he learned that when she'd had emotional challenges they manifested in bodily problems. She never had to say a word to him for the reactions in her body were obvious: worry on her face, fitful sleep, poor appetite that usually ended up in anemia, stomach problems with vomiting, bouts of dehydration, and exhaustion. He had a keen intuitive sense; when someone was really ill the hackles on the back of his neck would raise and his gut instinct was rarely wrong. He was well aware of the town talk lately and the situation with her and Charley, and knew how this must be affecting her. He also knew the two women were tight, even contemplated from time to time how involved they were with each other; a thought he would never let see daylight. Mildred's beneficence, loans turned into subsidies to a lot of people, including him when he needed medical supplies, was not lost on him. She never turned anyone down no matter how they treated her. His return kindness was to hold her and Edra in a safe place and do whatever he could to be supportive of their needs.

"She feels defeated."

"Over all that nonsense?"

"People don't take to her. All the ridicule over the years. If some-thing happens to her, I have nobody," she sobbed.

"Hey there. Hey now, you're getting way ahead of yourself. And it's not true that nobody likes her. Why Frank Whitmore just told me some mighty nice things about Mildred. And Charley. They struck up a nice friendship. Charley don't take to just anybody. He's a good man, that Charley."

"You think so?"

"You bet. Minds his business, helps the children at the school, was devoted to his Emma. Don't come better than Charley Milpass. He sat beside Mildred when Pursey brought her in. Wouldn't leave her side till she came to. If you got two friends in this world, you're lucky. Plenty people know they'd be out of business, hard up, were it not for Mildred's support."

"I don't know about Charley, and the people in this town are so mean to her."

"So what? She's strong. Been through it before with town stupidity. It'll pass and you'll be just fine. Charley's been in my place just about every day asking after her. He doesn't say much but Emma's death was hard on him." He made a point to emphasize, "He's pretty tight-lipped. Seems genuinely concerned about Mildred."

"He has?" Her demeanor changed with that information. *But why is he still paying so much attention to her? That's what worries me. Have I misjudged him?* "I'm just worried about Mildred."

"Sure you are, Edra. So now tell me what's been going on with Mildred."

"Pretty much what I told you."

"Physically. Nothing else? Pain? Vomiting? Fever?"

"Not sure about the fever with all the sweating at night." Then she remembered, "A while back, maybe a few weeks, she vomited brown specks."

"Has that happened again since then?"

"Not that I know of. I'd forgotten all about that till you asked. Think she had a nose bleed the night before."

"I wouldn't worry about it if it was just that one time. Could have also been a burst capillary from vomiting. If it continues let me know. As for the sweating at night, it's also been overly hot," he replied. "How much is she actually eating and drinking?"

Edra told him what Mildred had consumed over the last twenty-four hours.

"And the last week?"

She told him.

"That's not going to kill her. She might lose some weight but really, it's okay what she's eating and even better she's drinking enough."

Edra asked, "Do you want to see her now?"

"Let her sleep. She probably needs it more than me waking her to figure out why she's not sleeping," he laughed. "I've got to come back out here tomorrow to see the Whitmore's baby. I'll stop in on you then. You're clearly doing your job, getting what nourishment you can into her."

"Doesn't seem like enough to me."

"You got good motherly instincts but believe me, she's a long way from starving."

"Okay. If you say so." She wanted to say more, changed her mind, then thanked him.

"You bet. You take care now. And my suggestion to you," he held up his cup of tea, "more chamomile tea for you. Help you relax."

Doc said his good-byes and left with the thought that he should stop by and see Charley on his way home.

"So, how's she doing?" Charley's voice cracked.

"I think a visit from you would be a darn good thing for her."

Charley took a relaxed breath. "You sure?"

"Yeah, and Charley, I wouldn't involve anyone else in your business with Mildred."

"Don't plan to, Doc." He contemplated, *Once you put it out there, there's no taking it back. No way I'm gonna contribute to the insanity already afoot.* "Learned long ago to keep my mouth shut and pay attention."

Doc patted Charley on the back. "Good."

*

Charley fell asleep that night while reading *Nature* by Emerson. The next morning, as he moved in his sleep, the book fell to the floor with a thud and woke him. His eyes opened to the sun flooding in through his bedroom window, and he smiled, feeling refreshed after the first good night's sleep he had had in many days. He jumped out of bed, got dressed, and made himself a bite to eat.

Charley whistled to himself in anticipation as he rode out for a visit with Mildred.

Edra answered Charley's knock at the door with a surprised look.

"You're not expecting me?" he asked.

"No."

"Doc told me to stop by."

"Oh he did, did he?" She was just about to send him away when she noticed a book in his hand. "You came here to give us that?"

"I'm reading this. Thought we could talk about it."

Edra surprised herself with a nervous laugh. She was torn between her suspicions of his intentions toward Mildred and a feeling inside that he was a good person just trying to be friends with them. She thought for a minute about the last time they discussed books, and changed her mind about him staying. "Okay, Charley. Have a seat out there. I'll get Mildred."

Mildred was resting on the bed. "I heard you talking to someone. Who's here?"

"Before you react, Doc told him to come. And it might not be a bad idea."

"Charley?"

Edra smiled. "He brought a book with him to talk about."

"I don't want to."

Edra urged, "What's the harm? You're the one always tells me to face things."

"I don't have the energy to argue with you, Edra."

"Then don't. Come on out. Let's hear what he's been reading."

"A woman can't get herself any rest," she mumbled, following Edra to the porch.

Charley noticed how gaunt Mildred's face looked. "Mildred."

"Hi Charley."

"I see you brought *Nature* with you," said Edra. "Emerson used to be a minister. Claims it is possible to reach spiritual states without organized religion."

"That's what you're reading?" asked Mildred, "About religious…" She stopped and made a gesture to get up and leave.

"Wait! Don't go," begged Charley. "There's more to it. Emerson emphasizes studying and responding to the natural world. Gus said he heard him lecture once. When I'm done with this, I want to read *Walden*."

Edra asked with interest "How come you chose these two?"

"Gus says that *Walden* talks about resistance to meddlesome dictates in organized society. I think those were Gus's words. I had no idea what he was talking about. He wouldn't answer when I asked, instead told me to read these books."

"Does it make sense to you now?" asked Edra.

"I haven't read *Walden* yet but I know that Emerson was a student of Thoreau."

"Thoreau lived by himself for two years in a cabin in the woods by a pond," Mildred commented. "His writing was radical."

"Radical?" asked Charley.

"He expresses a deep-rooted tendency toward individualism," responded Mildred.

Edra joined in. "Yes, as opposed to a crowd and political mentality."

Mildred's cheeks took on a slightly rosier complexion. Edra relaxed as she saw Mildred's energy perking up.

"Gus is a tricky guy," Mildred laughed.

"How so?" asked Charley.

"After our last go round in town he's got you reading these things. I'd say that was clever."

"Got another one he said I must read."

Edra asked, "Which one?"

"*The Scarlet Letter.*"

"What!" Edra blushed.

Charley asked, "You read it?"

"Yes, we both have," said Mildred.

The women laughed.

"Did Gus tell you what it's about?" asked Mildred.

"No."

Mildred smiled with embarrassment. "It's about a woman cast out of her community for committing adultery. Some religious people think it's immoral to read it."

Edra looked preoccupied. "I think *The Scarlet Letter* and *Uncle Tom's Cabin* were both banned around the time of the Civil War."

"Yes, they were," said Mildred.

"Well then, I guess Gus has me reading some interesting books," Charley said.

"I'd say so," laughed Edra.

Mildred smiled and asked Edra, "How's about something to drink. Charley, would you like something?"

By the time Doc returned in the late afternoon, Mildred was up and helping with the usual household routines. Edra met up with him by his carriage. "Thanks."

He looked puzzled.

"For telling Charley to stop by."

"And Mildred?"

"It helped get her mind off...you know."

Doc put his hand on hers. "Always welcome good news."

"We are all in the gutter, but some of us are looking at the stars." OSCAR WILDE

22

Three days passed since Charley's visit and despite the fact that Mildred felt better she still did not want to go to town and have to stomach running into Josie, Pat, or any of the other women involved in the recent upset. Although most of the town seemed to be well over the gossip about Charley and Mildred, for Josie and her group there was no letting up. Doc had inadvertently fueled the flame when he was overheard in Gus's store ordering a herbal remedy for female problems. Madeline was in the store at the time and was familiar with the medicine. Since she knew that Doc had recently gone to Mildred's and had not heard of anyone else in town suffering from anything similar, she leaped to the conclusion that it must be for Mildred. It never entered her mind that it was also used for relief of non-pregnancy nausea and vomiting, which is what Doc used for the Whitmore's baby.

"We haven't seen Mildred around here for ages," she said to Josie and Hanah later as she described what she had heard in Gus's store.

"What was it that he ordered?" asked Josie.

"Same herbal remedy that Doc prescribed for me when I cramped up with my first child."

Josie slapped her hand on her lap. "Why, that homely hag. I knew it! That's it! We are going there to see Mildred once and for all."

"How you going to swing that?" asked Madeline.

"I have an idea. But first we need to pay Helene a visit."

Hanah was puzzled. "Why Helene? What do you have in mind, Josie?"

Josie pushed away the chair she was sitting on, then grabbed her bag and sweater. "I'll explain it on the way," she said to the two women.

She did so as they rode out to the Whitmore's ranch. "If Frank's there, just make idle talk till we can get Helene alone."

"Well, we'll see what Helene has to say about it, I guess," said Hanah with some doubt after hearing Josie's idea.

Helene listened to what Josie had to say about all of them paying Mildred a visit and felt nervous. She did not want to go against Josie but was afraid if she went along with her she'd further upset Frank. "I don't know. Got my hands full with the baby."

"It wouldn't be a long visit. Let's have a look at the baby." She started to push her way past Helene into the house.

"Wait! He's sleeping. He is doing better, but I have to keep an eye on him. Can't leave him…"

"We can take him with."

Helene squirmed. "I don't have the time to make a pie and all."

"Hanah can make the pie." Josie shot Hanah a look.

"Yes, of course. I'll do it," said Hanah.

Helene's gut churned. At a loss for any further excuses and with great reluctance she asked Josie, "Why do you even need me to go with you? Frank warned me to keep out of Mildred's…"

"You're the one that goes out there, aren't you?"

"Well no, Frank does when he pays the rent."

"I mean of us women," snapped Josie.

"Oh, yes of course, when Frank can't." Just then she heard her baby crying in the other room. "Excuse me a minute."

"That Helene is so dumb," Josie whispered to Madeline and Hanah. "Why the hell does she think we came all the way out here?" Helene walked back carrying little Frankie. "Helene," Josie smiled, "we need you to go. You just tell them you decided to visit with a fresh-baked pie to pay your respects, and asked us to come along for support. Be too suspicious without you."

"I don't know…"

"We can't do it without you!" Josie hammered.

⁕

On the day of the visit, Josie arrived at Hanah's just as she removed the pie from the oven. "It'll cool on the way to Helene's," Hanah assured her.

"Where is everyone?" Josie was annoyed.

"You're early."

"No, I'm not." Josie paced and fumed until Sarah and Annalee arrived five minutes early. "About time."

The two women gave each other a look.

⁕

Helene, sweating up a storm, was standing outside when they arrived. She took one look at the expression on Josie's face and shrank into herself. "I got the baby to a sitter," she stammered. "Worked out okay. Frank's gone to Walker Junction."

"The baby's better?" asked Sarah.

"Never mind all that. Let's go." Josie commanded.

The women were uncharacteristically quiet as they rode to Mildred's place, each imbued in her own thoughts, Josie in an excited anticipation while Helene was freaking out, desperately trying to calm herself. She tried to get her attention off the nagging feeling that what they were doing would come to no good. She wanted to turn around and go home but worse, she feared any reaction she might get from Josie were she to say anything. When she saw the Dunlap's ranch surface over the last hill they turned on, she felt ill.

⁕

Thinking that it was Charley when she heard a knock, Edra nearly fell over when she opened the door.

"We heard Mildred was ill, so we brung her this." Josie handed her the pie.

Helene, feeling uncomfortable with the edge in Josie's voice, joined

160

in. "Didn't think you would mind us bringing this to you."

Hanah and Sarah nodded. Annalee fidgeted with her fingernails.

Edra, still dumbfounded, could not utter a word.

Josie, in a sickeningly sweet manner spoke. "Is Mildred here? We'd love to see her."

Edra found her tongue, but stumbled over her words. "She's resting."

"Mind if we wait? Can we come in?" Josie stepped in closer to Edra.

"This is not a good time. I appreciate your effort but she needs her rest. Thank you, ladies. Now if you'll excuse me."

Josie blocked the door so it wouldn't close.

Helene, on reflex reacted, "Josie!"

Josie shot Helene a dirty look then turned to Edra, "We just wanted Mildred to know we were here. Sure do hope she's okay. Just wanted to pay our respects." Josie tried to suppress her animosity and act concerned in order to get through the door.

An annoyed Edra would have none of it. "I'll let her know. Now if you'll excuse me."

Helene nervously nudged Josie's leg with her foot indicating that that was enough. Josie reluctantly stepped back. "Well, all right. How about we come back another time?" Helene asked as she also backed away. "Sorry for any inconvenience."

"If you'll excuse me now…" Edra started to close the door.

Josie broke in. "We'll come around again to see how things are."

Edra stood by the closed door fuming. *What nerve! Haven't you all done enough!* It was all she could do to contain herself from screaming. She went to the kitchen and dumped the pie in the garbage.

On their way to drop off Helene, Sarah commented, "Mildred must really be ill."

Annalee added, "She never even showed her face."

Josie laughed. "She's just too far along and doesn't want anyone seeing her."

Helene was silent.

*

Edra was still stunned when she went back to check up on Mildred, who was in a deep sleep. As she watched Mildred breathe, the aftershock of the visit sank in, filling her with a horrific reminder of the first time she felt threatened, just after the rape. She sensed the sickening pleasure Josie had in violating the boundary of her privacy with Mildred, just like her rapist took pleasure in forcing his way on her. To her there was no difference between then and now, except for the blood and physical pain. Out of nowhere she thought of their dog, Chessie, who was killed by a rattler. She found it curious why that came up until she felt the fear she experienced watching her dog squirm to a horrible death. The same fear ran through her after the rape, only then it wasn't the fear of a snake but all mankind. She sat by Mildred, watching her chest motion rise and fall, till her insides began to calm. Just as she was about to walk out she heard Mildred mumble, "Harold, Bert, run..."

At first Edra had no idea what the mumbling was about, then she heard her say, "The Parker boys did it," and she knew exactly what Mildred's nightmare was. The next thing that happened startled her. Mildred moaned with a smile on her face, "Charley." That's the last thing she expected, that Mildred would be calling out for Charley. *Is it the truth coming out of you now? We don't lie when we're sleeping! I knew it. Goddamnit all to hell!*

By some inexplicable coincidence, as if fate had picked this day to test her limit for torment, Charley arrived at the door with a bag of groceries. "Mildred?" he called.

Mildred didn't stir.

Edra went to the door in a huff. "Who told you to come with those!"

"I thought you could use..."

Without letting him finish, she stormed out.

He watched her run toward a field a ways from the house, then decided to find her. When he did she was huddled on the ground under intertwining trees, screaming in grief. He stood at a distance to give her some room to calm down before approaching. When the screams became louder he wondered if he should turn around and leave until he heard her utter a desperate howl. "Why! She loves Charley!"

Charley, not sure what to do, stayed put. *How could you think Mildred loves me? She doesn't even want me around.* He reflected back to what he had started to imagine a few days earlier. *It's true what I thought…how you two watch over each other, the tenderness, the way you touch each other. The one bed! How could I have been so stupid? I see in you two what I had with Emma. Oh God, what am I going to do with this?* It mattered not that he was aware then that Mildred had been using him, for he knew that in protecting love all things were fair. He would have stopped at nothing for Emma. He remembered his conversations with Gus, who expounded on the hatred that Wilde's imprisonment engendered. He also recalled the incident years earlier with the Parker boys, which made him feel a deep sorrow, an empathy that was new for him. It gave him strength, an inner knowing, that if he were honest it would set things straight. He approached her delicately and when he was behind her, spoke very softly. "There's nothing between me and Mildred."

Edra bolted up to face him. "What are you doing here? Leave me alone."

He very gingerly responded. "I'm not the one she loves."

Edra could not believe her ears. "What?"

"Edra. Let me help you. Let's take you back. You've got nothing to worry about. Hope you know I'm a friend.

"You're not my friend! Ever since she took up with you it's brought us nothing but heartache. Leave me alone!"

He knew there was truth to this statement. He also knew that Mildred's interest was a diversion. The pieces that had not made sense were now falling into place. He stood before her hushed, refusing to move.

Edra broke down in tears. When he reached to comfort her she backed away, still unable to speak or stop crying.

"I don't want to bring any more upset to you or Mildred. Maybe that's why she called my name. She knows I'm a friend." He put a hand on her elbow. This time she did not try to move away. She listened as he continued. "I've been grateful to have a friend. I thought that's what

Mildred wanted also. There's absolutely nothing between us, other than that."

"You overheard me…and you…don't want to …" she muttered.

"No, Edra. For me Emma was it."

"There's really nothing with you and Mildred?"

"Oh, there's something but not what you're afraid of. She's been kind to me."

Edra felt embarrassed. "Oh my God. What did I just do!"

Charley took her by the shoulders. "Listen to me. There's no hurt going to come from me to you, or to Mildred. I know what it is to love. And I sure as hell know what it is to hurt. I have no intention of bringing any harm to either of you."

Edra saw the honesty in his eyes, felt it in her body. She wanted to believe what he was saying. She remembered what Doc had said about him. But she was so deeply wounded that she could trust no one beside Mildred. "I just don't trust you."

"I don't blame you. That's gonna take time. There's been so much meddling. Been hard for us to just get to know each other. I sure do hope, with time, you'll learn to trust me." His eyes welled up with tears. "Got my own pain I'm dealing with. My friendship with Mildred…and Gus…and the kids at school…means the world…"

She saw and understood what he was trying to say but it was more from what he was not saying, how his voice was tender and the expression on his face so filled with deep hurt, that spoke to her and momentarily calmed some of the fear.

"Charley…I…I just can't…" She didn't know how to respond.

"It's okay. No need to say anything else. I'll be getting now and let you be."

She looked at him with tears flowing down her cheek.

"There is just one more thing." With a gentle understanding smile, he continued, "I'm going to do my best to show you I am your friend."

"Wisdom comes with winter." Oscar Wilde

23

The relief Edra felt with Charley was quickly replaced with worry. She was inexperienced in matters involving relationships outside of Mildred, yet felt there was something speaking to her that told her experience was irrelevant when it came to her inner voice, the sense inside that sat right with her. She knew when she first felt something for Mildred that it was safe to pursue it. She knew, just as the sunset gave way to darkness, there was a natural order to everything. She sensed it around Ben, who worked for the Dunlaps as far back as she could remember, with Doc who never betrayed them, and today this same feeling arose with Charley out in the meadow. All that did nothing to stop the doubt from arising that maybe she let too much slip. Up came the image of Josie at her door and flashes of too many times Mildred was upset over the turmoil her feigned interest in Charley had created. By the time she arrived back at the bedroom to find Mildred waking, she was scared she'd opened a can of worms. "You had a good long sleep. Good that you're catching up." She didn't want to hit Mildred with what happened all at once. "How you feeling?"

"Yeah, getting some rest sure helped. I had the weirdest dream."

"About the Parker boys?" Edra's stomach fluttered at the thought of mentioning Charley.

"No, why would you bring up them?"

"You were moaning their names in your sleep."

"Huh, I don't remember that one. The one I was aware of was about Charley. Very strange, like a fairy tale. He was on a horse and came to rescue us. He found out about us…"

Edra had a hard time focusing on what Mildred said.

"…he disappeared. I looked all over for him, to thank him. That's when I woke up."

Edra wiped moisture from her forehead and tried to speak but burst into tears.

"Why are you crying?" Mildred sat up.

"Mil, I've done something."

"What?"

The blood drained from Edra's face. Her mouth felt like she'd been sucking cotton. "I told Charley."

"What?"

"I told him. Well, not exactly, he overhead me."

Mildred winced. "What are you saying?"

"He was here."

Mildred waited for her to continue.

"I hope I didn't mess things up."

"Just tell me."

"I couldn't help it. I heard you calling out for Charley. I thought maybe you…I was so upset. It was just after Helene came by with Josie."

That jolted Mildred. "Josie was here! And Helene! For God's sake, why?"

"To bring you a pie. They wanted to see you. Josie was obnoxious. I don't want to talk about them!" With the mention of Josie's name, Edra felt shame over what happened with Charley. *What if he says something to them?*

Difficult as it was to quell her anger, Mildred calmed herself. "Okay, go on."

Edra relayed the events up to the part where she screamed about Mildred loving Charley…"

"What's wrong with that?"

Edra became hysterical. "It just came out. I couldn't help it. I didn't know he was there."

"Hey. Hey. Hey there, come here." Mildred patted the bed. "Come sit by me."

Edra cried and talked till she finished telling Mildred what happened.

"That's it? That's what you're all upset about?" She wanted to soothe Edra.

"How come you're taking this so well?"

Mildred smiled. "We don't really know exactly what he thinks or not. Lot of family love each other."

"He equated it with his love for Emma. I'm telling you he knows."

"Love is love. Everybody knows I love you as family. Been taking care of you for years. That's been the story. Probably what he's thinking."

"I don't think so, Mil."

"Well, look, we really don't know for sure. Tell me about Josie."

"Oh, they made me so mad. They brought a pie. Josie was despicable. I swear, she almost ran over me to get into the house…"

"What! She came into our home!"

"No, she didn't make it past Helene." She went on to tell what else transpired. "She gave me the willies."

Mildred was disgusted with what she heard. "Now you see why we needed this distraction with Charley."

"I hope I didn't give him the impression."

"From what you told me, don't worry. We just need to be more careful."

"I'm so sorry, Mil."

*

While Mildred and Edra discussed and reviewed their options, Charley stopped by Gus's on his way home, where a light shone through a single window upstairs. He tossed a small pebble at it. Gus came to the window, saw it was Charley, and went downstairs. "What brings you here at this hour?"

"Think I can have a drink?"

"Sure, Charley. Come on in."

"Let me give you something for the booze. Must be costing you a pretty penny."

"Don't worry about it, Charley."

They went upstairs and Gus poured drinks. "Here ya go. What's on your mind?"

Charley downed the shot and held up his glass for another. Gus pushed the bottle over to him.

"Got something going through my head."

Gus didn't respond, waiting for Charley to continue.

"My parents taught me things. Ministers too. Was raised Protestant. Never questioned my faith till recently. Now, not sure what's what. People say things are in the Bible about what's right and wrong. But I don't feel some of these things are wrong. Does that make me a bad Christian?"

"God gave you a brain, Charley. If you're using it then that's a gift from him. Not for someone else to determine for you what's right and wrong. Twenty people read the Bible and each has a different interpretation. More wars fought and blood shed over religion than anything else. That should tell you something. No clear right or wrong about anything. That's how I see it."

"Why was everybody in such a huff over that Wilde fellow?" asked Charley. "Do you think people are really bothered over it? Do you think it's wrong, Gus?"

"Wrong? No."

"You're serious? You weren't raised to think a man with a man is wrong?"

"How I was raised is irrelevant. It's how I feel now. What do I believe now? What has experience taught me? Have I used my head to look for myself? Or am I a puppet to someone else's ideas? I can think for myself. Same sex together don't bother me at all."

"What brought you to feeling that way?"

"Guess I got lucky."

"Huh?"

"Yeah, somewhere along the line I learned to think for myself. I question things. Ask myself if it's true…or just someone's idea?"

"How can you tell if anything's true?"

"Don't know that I, or anyone for that matter, can ever answer that. That's been a burning question for centuries."

"Well, then…" Charley downed his shot. "How come it doesn't bother you?"

"Can't answer that either. Just know that I try to look at things with an open mind. Not judge. Can I just see things for what they are, not what I want them to be or what others tell me they are but what do I actually see or experience myself?"

"Like what?"

"Well, let's take the Wilde situation. What was that really all about? Way I see, it was an extension of nature; whatever their reason for wanting to be together they wanted it. Who got hurt by it? What human being doesn't want for something? We're all human. Have our desires, needs, habits, the good, the bad, all of it. I don't see myself as any different from anyone else as far as my insides."

This perplexed Charley. "I don't understand that at all. To me, you're so different than…"

"Oh sure, on one level there are differences but in terms of understanding human beings we all have emotions and desires. What differs is our experiences. The stuff that gets put in our heads from others. From the minute we're born we're told what to think."

"Yeah, so how does one get to…"

"Don't really know. I don't think there's any how to get to, no switch to turn on, or turn off anything. Not really."

Charley scratched his head. "I don't get what you're saying."

"You know the expression, there by the grace…?"

"Yeah."

"Well then, how come what happened to Wilde happened to him and not to someone else? How come Josie's family fell on hard times? How come Mildred keeps being persecuted? How did we come to be friends? It's all a mystery. So in that sense, suppose you have to ask God that question. Not just another human." Gus laughed.

"Do you ever find answers in the Bible?"

"Truth be told? It was written a hundred years after Jesus died. Can't quite comment on its accuracy," he smiled. "I'll tell you this much, there's a lot of wisdom in it if you understand the parables and what they are attempting to teach. But ultimately, I don't find comfort in referring to anything written. I like to rest in my own experience. What I find is true, or rather real, for me.

"But isn't the point of sex to have children?"

Gus became frustrated that he wasn't getting through. "Come on, Charley, you think we can control who we're attracted to?"

"Don't need to act on it."

"And live a life without intimacy? Never to know what it is to make love? Look at all the pain come to Wilde. Do you think he chose that? Don't you think he would have changed if he could have?"

Charley was feeling dizzy. "Think I've had enough." He put the cap on the bottle and pushed it back to Gus. "Thanks for this. I'll tell ya Gus, right now I don't know what I feel is right or wrong. Am pretty confused. I see someone loving someone and remember how it was with me and Emma. Can never find anything wrong with that. Then I get other ideas that tell me it's not right."

"Boy, I understand that. Just remember, ideas can kill."

"Whhhhhaaaat?"

"You get an idea in your head about something being wrong, get into a fight over it to defend your point, on and on and on and we end up killing someone because of an idea. Throw someone in prison because of another idea. Look at it!"

Charley had stopped by Gus's hoping to sort things out, but their conversation was only adding to his confusion. "It's getting late, Gus. I don't want to be taking up any more of your time."

Gus got up and went over to his nightstand, picked up a piece of paper, and handed it to Charley. "I was reading Aristotle today. Wrote down something I wanted to share with you."

Charley took the folded piece of paper and put it in his shirt pocket.

"Thanks for letting me come talk. And the drinks. Think I'm more mixed up now than when I come."

"Not surprising, Charley. Give it time."

*

Charley, up through most of the night, mulled over ideas, impressions, opinions, beliefs he had held all his life, now all a jumble. Nothing made sense. The thoughts continued until clouds rolled out of the sky and the sun ushered in morning, filling his room with light. He realized that he could think himself to death and never find an answer to anything and saw with clarity that the only certainty was uncertainty, that when he questioned something it changed. In a paradoxical way he saw that the only thing that was stable in time was change.

The next day, exhausted and dispassionate, he watched more thoughts float through without anchor, like migrating birds. When no more came, he watched his attention shift from the cumulus fluffs of condensed water in the sky, to drops of dew on pieces of grass, to ants carrying twigs twice their body size. He became aware of something that he had never noticed before: life without thinking, no thoughts or beliefs dictating his actions. He saw life in motion and all that was left of him was involved in this movement. He continued to look around until he remembered the note that Gus had given him and pulled it out of his shirt pocket. It read: "Without friends no one would choose to live, though he had all other goods. Aristotle 384–322 B.C." He no longer felt confused or without direction.

"Consistency is the last refuge of the unimaginative."
OSCAR WILDE

24

Josie and her five friends in cahoots met for tea at Barney's Cafe to formulate a new Mildred plan.

"Did you get a look at her?" asked Madeline.

"No," replied Josie.

"So, if you do another 'make a pie and don't get to see her,' what's the point?"

Josie replied with a cocky confidence. "We'll just make sure we get in to see her this time."

Barney was working the cafe alone with the cook. He watched the group of women chat away and reflected back to a conversation with his wife, Pat:

"Josie made me look like a fool."

"You were ripe to look like a fool!"

Pat threw a dishrag at him. "Why would you say something like that?"

"You sit around yipping with your lady friends. Don't know if there's a lick of truth to any of your chattering, yet you're ready to pass along a bunch of junk."

"I didn't make it up, Barney. What're you getting all over me for?"

"Might as well have. You listen to Josie's blabbing. That woman

makes a life out of getting into others' hair. Better watch out, woman, or it'll be you next."

"She's my friend."

"That's some friend you got there, Pat. You'd do better to keep to yourself and mind your manners."

Barney watched the group banging their lips together, the volume rising, and was glad Pat was not there.

"Mildred won't stay in her room forever," said Sarah.

"When's Frank going back to Walker Junction?" Josie looked at Helene.

Helene replied, "Two days, but I don't want to do that again."

Josie reproved her. "We're not going without you. That'd ruin everything."

Annalee joined in. "You're the only one of us that has any business going over there."

Helene felt cornered. "Frank does the…"

Josie hammered onto her. "You said you go there sometimes. You told Edra…You're the one that started all this and now you're backing down!" Her voice grew louder. "You came around in the first place with all the Charley talk. How he's so happy now, babysitting for you, and you were happy about him and Mildred. You were quick to involve yourself when you thought you could win favor with Mildred to get at some of her money."

Helene sank lower in her chair.

Sarah tried to soften the blows. "Helene, if you make the pie it'll be hot when we arrive. Who can refuse a freshly baked pie?"

"I just can't." shuddered Helene.

Josie struggled to control her anger. "Nonsense. We need a warm pie to get us in the door. You're the only one who lives close enough. You want us to go there without you and make it look like you don't care about Mildred? Think, woman! We can't do it without you. You make one of your pies so it's warm. Leave the rest up to me."

Helene, too intimidated to speak, nodded agreement. It was the same domination she felt from her father, how he bullied, threatened, browbeat, and finally had his way with her. Through the years, she learned that the more she resisted the worse it became, so she catered to him, propitiated, until she was old enough to entice another man to get what she wanted, which was to leave her home. It became her way, when threads of the torture arose in her triggered by some similar aspect, that she cowered and condescended. Josie's attitude and forcefulness had that effect on her.

"That'll work!" Sarah said loudly.

Josie snapped, "Quiet down."

Madeline, who had sat quietly through their conversation, whispered, "This is exciting. I can't wait to get out there to find out what's going on with Mildred."

"Okay, well then. Two days." Josie concluded the conversation then flagged down Barney who had been standing by the counter in earshot of their conversation. They paid him and left.

Later that afternoon when Pat arrived at the cafe, he said to her, "Your friends are at it again. They just don't let up. Good thing you weren't here. Hey, where'd that come from?" He looked at the floor where Pat was heading. "Watch where you're...Pat!"

She skidded on a wet spot, landing backside down, with the bag of salt she was holding flying all over the floor.

"Pat! That's the last of the salt!"

"I'll go get more," she cowered.

Barney jumped in. "I'll do it! After all that squawking, I need some fresh air. You clean that mess up." He helped her up and made his way out. Across the street, he ran into Sheriff Roper. "Hey Roper, things quiet for you?"

"Yeah. That's how I like it. You?"

"The hens were at it again. I needed a breather."

Roper laughed.

"Be seeing ya." Barney continued on down the street to Gus's and was glad that other than one other male customer, the store was empty. "Hey, Gus."

"Barney."

Barney made his way to the noticeboard to see if there were any new telegrams that had come in. There was nothing since the last one posted about Olney and President Cleveland. Disappointed, he said to Gus, "Nothing new on the board there? I'll be needing a bag of salt. The big one."

"No. No telegrams today. How's business, Barney?" Gus asked as he procured the bag of salt.

"Oh, you know. The chatterboxes are keeping me in clothes," he laughed.

"Come again?"

"The girls are banging their mouths. Man, they just don't give it a rest."

"What now?"

"Josie was on a tirade about bringing Mildred a pie. Pushing hard on Helene to go along with it." He continued to express his repugnance for what happened. "They're all in this huddle over a goddamn fresh pie that Helene has to bake. Thought she was going to pass out. They need to find something else to do with their lives. But enough of that. Came over here to get away from that nonsense."

Gus shook his head to indicate he understood. "Some things never change." He gave Barney a pat on the back. "I'll put this on your tab."

Gus knew that no good was afoot. Later that day when he closed shop, he walked over to Charley's to express his concerns so he could forewarn Mildred.

*

It was dark out when Charley arrived at Mildred's. When she saw him at the door it gave her a bad feeling. "I asked you to please let us know before you popped in on us. This is getting to be too much."

"I appreciate that, Mildred. I wouldn't be here if it wasn't important."

The look on his face made her very uneasy. "Charley, it's late."

Edra approached behind Mildred, saw Charley and got scared. "What's going on?"

Mildred said to Charley, "Wait there a minute." She moved Edra back from the door and whispered, "It'll be okay. I'll handle this."

"No. Tell him to come in. I want to hear what's going on."

Mildred let him in and they all sat in the living room. "Go on, Charley."

"I heard something disturbing today."

Mildred saw Edra flinch. "If you've come here to make trouble then I think you better leave before you let any unkind words pass between us."

Edra moaned, "I shouldn't have said…"

"You think I'm here about the other day?"

Edra nodded.

"Oh no, not at all. Since that came up I wanted to tell you both, I've been thinking…don't quite know how to say this. I had a talk with Gus…"

"You said something to Gus?" Edra gasped.

Mildred shot her a look that said, *Watch what you say.*

"No. He just helps me get clarity on my thinking. I really want you both to know I'm your friend. No question about it. I hope you…"

Mildred was perturbed with the idle chatter. "Get to the point please."

"Okay, but it's important you understand where I'm coming from."

Mildred's patience was threadbare. "What did you hear that you came to tell me?"

"I think Josie is planning on something to embarrass you." He directed that comment to Mildred. "Her friends are in on it, including Helene."

"In on what?" asked Mildred, still annoyed that he wouldn't just get to the point.

He relayed what Gus had told him with the emphasis on Josie corralling the women into going along with her. "Barney was pretty aggravated by the carrying on."

Edra continued, "This is why you came out here?"

"Yes."

"What did you hope to achieve by coming here, Charley?" asked Mildred.

"If you know what's happening you can prepare yourself. They're planning on coming over in a couple days."

"They already came by and nothing happened. We'll just ignore them," said Mildred.

"Josie won't stop till she sees you. So I thought I could be here."

Edra asked "Why?"

Charley's face turned red. "Let them see us together. You know…"

At that moment both Mildred and Edra understood what Charley was offering.

Mildred spoke softly and with caution. "You're assuming there'll be trouble here without you being present. I've handled my life up till now by myself. Think I can handle a flock of busybodies coming around."

Charley only knew one way to be and that was honest. He also knew that Gus wouldn't have come over to his place without strong concern. To Charley's gut this was trouble brewing and he felt responsible for setting it in motion because of his friendship with Mildred. He knew Mildred was being protective and not of any mindset to trust anything coming from him, and so he spoke from everything in him that said he had to. "I have a really bad feeling about what I heard. I can't just walk away from you. I've caused you so much grief by wanting to be friends…"

Mildred saw where this was heading. "How do we know we can trust you? How do I know you aren't involved in some way to make me look foolish?"

"I don't expect you to trust me. Told Edra the other day that takes time. But I can say this…" His eyes filled with tears. "I swear on the grave of my dead wife, I don't intend to bring either of you any harm. I'm here offering my friendship. You decide if you want to make a leap of faith and let me help you."

Mildred had to admit to herself the consistency of his sincerity that had shown in his eyes and had sat well in her gut. "So if we do go along with what you're proposing…"

"No! I don't trust him."

"I don't blame you, Edra. Maybe in time you will," said Charley.

Mildred looked over at Edra. "Let's just hear what he proposes."

"I'll just come around daily and plan on being here whenever they arrive. Let them think whatever they want about us. No harm to me. We can all just ride it out together."

"I don't know," Edra replied.

Mildred reached over to put a hand on Edra's. "That sounds reasonable to me."

"You want to go along with what Charley is suggesting?"

"Yes."

When he left, Edra asked Mildred, "Why'd you go along with him? It just solidifies what he thinks of us. It's exactly what we wanted to keep from others."

"Edra. What choice to do we have? We haven't told him anything. If he really does suspect what he alludes to, and he's really here to be a friend, under the circumstance what else could I have done?" Mildred knew she had to ride it out and if things did get out of hand they would have to leave. They were at a juncture: either choice could lead to heartbreak and devastation. All she had left was hope that Charley was a decent man. It killed her that she couldn't be sure.

"But..."

"Do you really think he's going to cause us trouble?"

"Oh God, I hope not."

*

There was more to Charley's idea than he let on to them. At five in the morning he awoke, got out of bed, dressed, and then quietly rigged up his horse and buggy. He hesitated a moment, trying to remember what else he needed to bring. *Rope. Where'd I leave that rope?* He arrived in Walker Junction at Josh Langford's an hour later and was in luck.

*

Edra had trouble sleeping so she got up early and milled around the kitchen making coffee while she found places to clean that hadn't gathered any new dust. She did not fully understand why she felt comforted when Charley pulled up at a little after light later that morning. The

178

minute she saw the load he'd brought, she understood why he had come.

He smiled. "I figure we can put this in the den. Think I remember there's a place in the back behind the desk?"

She listened. She knew then he must have seen the rooms the day she found him at the bedroom door.

"Don't want anyone rummaging around your place, getting wrong impressions. Been too much of that already."

"You did this for us?" Edra wasn't sure how to respond but was still not certain about him. "That couch is a little uncomfortable…"

"Sure it is, Edra."

Both knew what was left unsaid and that it was in the unspoken that a bond began to form between them. "Let me give you a hand." She helped him unload the mattress and frame. When the den was all set up, it looked like a lived-in second bedroom, and to Edra's surprise, was a great relief.

Just as they finished, the skies opened and a burst came from an early fall thunderhead, a scream that spoke for both of them. Then came the rains, a ferocious downpour that lasted no more than a few minutes. When it was all over, the air filled with freshness. Edra felt static electricity move through her and noticed it must have done the same with Charley, for the hair at the back of his head stood upright, which made her laugh.

"What?"

"Your hair," she continued laughing.

He joined her. "You too."

She turned to look at her reflection on the gun cabinet and saw she looked like a scared cat.

Mildred slept through the commotion, awakening to laughter. "No! Two eggs!" She was surprised to find them in the kitchen.

"Mildred!" Edra ran to her. "Come with me." Before Mildred could say a word or respond, she grabbed her hand and brought her to the den. The sun coming through the window cast a glimmer of light on the tears of relief streaming down Edra's cheeks.

"I told you he knows."

"Did he say anything?"

"No, and neither did I." She squeezed hold of Mildred's hand. "I told him the couch was not comfortable."

"So he'd think that's where you sleep…you're really okay with this?" One look at Edra, the light in her eyes, and she knew the question was rhetorical.

Edra smiled deep and long, then hugged her. "Mil, he reminds me of papa."

Just then, Mildred saw the light in the room grow brighter and turn a gentle blue. It embraced her body and sent a warm feeling from the base of her spine out through the top of her head. *Papa?*

They heard Charley, still out of earshot, singing in the kitchen.

"We teach people how to remember, we never teach them how to grow." OSCAR WILDE

25

Frank's plans to head out to Walker Junction early were thwarted when he went to check up on a cow with an infection on its nipple. The swelling had spread to its udder and if left untreated, it would cost them precious milk from one of his best producers. Helene rose early to peel apples and ready the dough for the pie she was to make when Frank returned from the barn. She was surprised to see him still home. "I thought you went to get the …"

"I'll have to do it tomorrow. We've got a sick one. Where'd you put that udder salve?"

Her heart just about stopped. *What am I going to do? The women will be here in an hour to go to Mildred's. Frank will kill me if he knows what we're planning. Salve? Where did I put it?*

She found it in a drawer and quickly hid it in her apron. "There's none here," she lied.

"How could that be? We just got a new tin."

She fumbled about pretending to look all over for it. "I can't find it."

He pushed her aside. "Let me have a look." He flung things around trying to find it. "Damn it, woman!" He threw a bag of bandages to the floor, followed by several other items till he had a clear view of all the contents in the drawer. "I'm gonna have to go to town." He gave Helene a disgusted look. "You need to keep better track of where you put things!"

She tried to steady her hands from shaking as she watched him take his time getting ready to leave. When he finally headed out the door she rushed to get Mabel out of bed. "Time to get up. Come on. Mamma's got a busy day." She had to hurry. If she gauged herself just right she'd have just enough time to get everything accomplished before everyone arrived, with the exception of taking the kids to the neighbor down the road to watch them. There was no time for that; they'd have to go with her to Mildred's.

Mabel moaned.

Helene shook her shoulder. "Wake up!" She pulled the covers down to Mabel's feet.

Mabel jumped up and laughed.

Helene was annoyed that Mabel was wasting time with games. "Come on, let's go eat. We've gotta get going."

"Where we going, mamma?"

Without responding, Helene took clothes out of the dresser and handed them to Mabel. "Here, now get yourself dressed, and be quick about it."

Mabel repeated, "Where we going?"

"To Mildred's."

"Can I bring Cranky?"

"Not today!" She saw Mabel lurch back at the harshness in her tone. "Let's go. Breakfast is waiting." Helene glanced at little Frankie asleep in his portable wood crib and returned to the kitchen with Mabel not far behind, still pulling on her clothes.

Mabel ate her breakfast while Helene readied the pie ingredients. *Oh man, I hope I'm ready in time.* She heard little Frankie's wake-up cry. She hurried to the bedroom, picked up his crib, and brought it to the kitchen. "Shhhhh, quiet down there," Helene said gently as he continued to fuss. She dipped a wooden baby spoon in sugar and put it in his mouth.

"When are we going?" Mabel whined.

THE PERSECUTION OF MILDRED DUNLAP

"I have to get this pie ready without any further interruptions. Go get your doll to play with."

Mabel jumped up and down. "Then we go? Then we go?"

"Mabel! Go get your doll! No more questions!"

Helene had finished preparing the apple mixture and started on the dough when little Frankie began fussing again. "Shhhh, quiet over there," she said absentmindedly, her attention preoccupied with the pie.

Mabel danced her doll around the floor making a loud clunking noise, which obscured a high-pitched soft whistling sound coming from the crib. Within seconds the sound turned into a barely audible wheeze.

Intent on the task at hand, Helene rolled out the pie dough and formed it in a pan.

Little Frankie began to flail in an effort to get air into his blocked windpipe, as Mabel kept banging away with her doll.

Helene poured the apple mixture onto the dough. She heard a gentle thump of the baby's body against the crib's mattress. It was a familiar sound that he made when tossing about in dreams.

"That's my good boy," she said, still with her back to the crib. She placed the pie in the oven, cleaned up and put away the leftover ingredients. Nearly eight minutes had passed between the last audible sound from Frankie and when Helene finally turned around to check on him. "You're being awfully good there, my little sweetie," she said as she watched Mabel playing. She reached down to pull the blanket back up over little Frankie, when her hand met his motionless body and she saw with alarm his lips were blue. Through her confusion, she saw that the edge of the spoon she had used to pacify him splintered off in his mouth. She grabbed her baby and screamed.

*

Cranky was barking incessantly while running in circles in the front yard as Josie and the others arrived.

"Who left that dog out? Those people are so irresponsible," complained Josie.

She and Madeline approached the front door first. "Something smells like it's burning," commented Madeline with a sniff.

Josie sarcastically replied, "Oh, that's just great."

The women filed through the door and stopped in confusion and shock to find Helene lying motionless on the floor with her dead baby clutched in her arms. Mabel stood next to her, sobbing in fear.

"Oh Lord!" screamed Annalee.

Sarah cried out, "Oh my God!"

Hanah stood with wide eyes, mouth agape in disbelief.

Josie froze, trying to comprehend what she saw when she felt a warm wind move through the room bringing with it a *rustle that sounded like the whisper of a magnolia. The flames grew higher, hotter, and the world turned dark and solemn. Everyone was screaming, no one making any sense. Her mamma found her and rushed her out of their home, never to return. She heard a new scream,* "Josie! Don't just stand there! Do something!" In a daze, she went to Helene who lay on the floor not moving, just staring into space.

Madeline yelled, "Lord help us!"

"What're we gonna do! What're we gonna do!" Annalee screeched.

Sarah, adjusting to the shock, went to Mabel. "Honey, why don't you come with me…"

"No! My mamma's sick. No!" She huddled against Helene.

Sarah remembered Mildred bringing Mabel to Charley's. "Hanah, go get Mildred. Tell her to come get Mabel."

Hanah rushed from the flurry, tripping over herself to get out the door, and rode as fast as she could to Mildred's. When Charley opened the door, she was unable to speak, trying to catch her breath, hyperventilating.

"It's just you?" he said, surprised.

"Charley!" she panted. "Thank the lord you're here. You need to get over to Helene's fast."

Suspicious, he asked, "What are you up to?"

Still short of breath, without thinking, she grabbed his arm. "You need to come with me. Helene! The baby! Oh my God…"

He pulled his arm back. "What the hell are you up to?"

She went white. "I think the baby's dead…little Frankie…"

Charley panicked. "What!"

"Please just come."

"I swear to you, Hanah…if this isn't on the up and up…"

"It's no joke. On my life. You need to come! We found Helene on the floor." She relayed what happened.

Mildred and Edra were in the bedroom when they heard Charley slam the front door and run to them. He urged, "Mildred, you need to come with me!" When she resisted, he continued with urgency, "There's something wrong with Helene and little Frankie! Hitch up Lil and follow me!"

"What if this is a trick?" she asked.

"Not the way Hanah's acting. Something terrible has happened. Let's go!"

Mildred knew not to question Charley further.

The three of them arrived at Helene's separately. Charley jumped from his buggy and ran into the house.

"Oh no!" he exclaimed as he saw the women surrounding Helene and the rigid body of his little nephew. He knew there was nothing he could do for little Frankie now and that Helene was in a nonresponsive state of shock. "Mabel, come here honey." He guided Mabel outside to Mildred. "Take her home with you."

Mildred saw the shock on Charley's face, and didn't question his demand.

"Come on, Mabel. Let's go do some baking at my place."

"My mamma's sick, Mildred. Maybe she should come too?"

"Uncle Charley will take care of your mamma, honey."

Charley watched them leave, then grabbed hold of Hanah who was still outside. "Stop standing there doing nothing and get your friends the hell out of here." He felt the retching rise in his gut. "For God's sake do something useful for once in your life and go tell Doc to get out here!"

Hanah ran into the house while Charley went behind a bush and vomited.

Josie didn't want to leave. Dazed and incoherent, she insisted, "Don't make me leave."

Charley took a couple of deep breaths. *What the hell is keeping them?* Entering the house, he was furious to hear Josie refusing to leave.

"You get that woman out of here and you do it now!" Charley yelled at Hanah.

Josie, still not making sense and not addressing her communication to anyone in particular, said, "I can't...leave my home. Don't make me leave."

Charley directed his attention to the group. "Get her out of here before I get my shotgun!"

Sarah and Madeline grabbed a hysterical Josie by her arms and dragged her out while she continued to mumble about not wanting to leave her home. The others quickly followed.

Charley went to Helene and the baby and knelt beside them. He touched little Frankie's lifeless cheek, still not believing what he saw, hoping he was wrong. Helene did not stir, her eyes still staring into space.

How'd this happen? Why?

He covered his face with his hands and broke down.

"The truth is rarely pure and never simple."

Oscar Wilde

26

A hush fell over Red River Pass as shock waves of the baby's death spread through town. Gasps of disbelief and tears from mothers filled the empty space created by the loss. No one was left unscathed by the news. Frank arrived home to find Charley waiting on the front porch, eyes bloodshot, looking dark and drawn. Doc, inside with a yet unresponsive Helene, heard Charley's attempt to say something that was interrupted by screams. Frank tore into the house and stopped dead in his tracks before his lifeless son. "No! No! This can't be…"

Doc stayed inside while Charley guarded the door from intruders. No one arrived with the exception of Amos who asked where Mabel was.

"At Mildred's."

"Is she going to stay there?"

"I'll get her and bring her and the dog over to my place," said Charley.

The men stayed at the door while Frank wailed till exhaustion took hold and he quieted down. Doc came out and the three men worked out the logistics.

Charley arrived at Mildred's close to midnight to find the women awake in the living room. Mabel was asleep on the new bed in the den,

Cranky by her side. Charley took one look at the peaceful innocent expression on her face and could not contain another burst of tears. No comfort was to be had, the pain too unbearable.

Mildred waited several minutes before going to Charley. She put a hand on his back and when he turned to face her she saw in him a look that put to rest any doubts she had about him, that he was a decent man, a sensitive man, and she had nothing to fear from him. She knew she had a friend in him and it pained her deeply that it took this horrible tragedy to show her what her heart had been unable to see in him earlier.

They went back out to Edra, who asked, "Would you like some tea, Charley?"

"No. Nothing. Don't think I could put anything in me just now. Wanted to…" He used his sleeve to wipe tears running down his cheeks, unable to continue.

Edra felt his sorrow. It was the first time in her life she felt anything for someone else outside of the Dunlap family, other than fear, and it moved her to speak. "Charley, let us know what we can do for you."

He nodded.

"For now, how about you sleep on the couch?" She looked to Mildred.

"Anything you need, we'll take care of whatever we can. Feel free to stay here as long as you like. We've plenty of food…"

"I don't want to put you two out anymore than…you've been way too kind bringing my niece here."

Mildred interrupted. "You're not going to wake up Mabel. We won't hear of you leaving now. You look exhausted."

"I agree with her, Charley. I wouldn't feel right with you leaving now."

He drew in a long slow breath, looked to Mildred, then Edra. "If you're sure it wouldn't be…"

"We're sure," said Mildred.

"Don't know how to thank you two. Not really sure how I'd of managed without your…"

Mildred saw how he was struggling, how sad he looked. "It's okay, Charley. We're here for you."

"Poor Frank. I don't know how he's going to get through this."

"Where is he?"

"Amos is staying there with him. Doc took…" The smothering heartache squeezed in on his chest.

"I'm so sorry." Edra moved over to him and put her hand on his. "I think what you need now is to try to get some rest."

Mildred spoke from her heart, in a softness only shared with Edra, when she said, "If it'll ease things a little, I want you to know I want to take care of helping Frank. I'll handle any expenses, anything he needs will be taken care of. We'll get Ben out to help over there till things settle down."

"You'd do that?" He was deeply moved by the offer. "But Ben's busy with your barn. You need him."

"All that can wait. Frank needs the help now."

Among the devastation and darkness, what she offered, a lull in the painful violence, a glimmer of hope, told him that with time things might return to normal. It was how he felt after Mildred brought Mabel around to his place for the first time. It was then he fully understood the beauty and value of their friendship.

✳

The service for little Frankie was held by the gravesite behind the church. The crowd gathered in shock, filling the small yard and over-flowing onto the street. Amos was up front next to Frank and the coffin, facing the crowd. Notably absent was Helene. Rebecca over at the Jenkins's place was watching her. Charley, Mildred, and Edra also stayed behind to tend to Mabel at the Dunlap's. Gus was there, standing at the back, in earshot of Satchel with Josie and their two boys.

Amos fought back tears as he looked around and saw Sam and Hanah with their children, Ben and Rose with theirs, Barney and Pat with their boys, and thought how the Whitmore's lives would forever be a family interrupted by tragedy. He came unprepared, knowing that words would never suffice. Although he was raised a Protestant, he believed in the Sacred Heart, and relied on it to guide him through times like this. When all else failed, his faith was a gift that did not let him down. He put an arm around Frank and silently called upon God to help him find the words of support for the devastated father standing beside him. He listened to muffled cries from breaking hearts, the shuffling of uncomfortable bodies struggling with their own emotions in the sweltering heat, and spoke. "How do we endure such a tragedy? Live with the unthinkable? The Lord God showed us the suffering we bestow upon each other as adults when he sent his Son to the cross, but...this...this was a baby. How do we begin to make sense of what happened? How do we call upon faith to..."

Frank stood solemn while at the back of the congregation Josie mumbled, "If Helene had been a better..."

Satchel squeezed her arm so tightly it stopped circulation. "Not here," he whispered back.

Gus, disgusted, took notice but said nothing. He felt a heaviness press in on him, making it near impossible to breathe, and an anger that was hard to contain. *That heartless bitch! Any sympathy I ever felt for you...you're not worth spit!* He was too preoccupied to hear anything more Amos said. *You'll get yours!* Whatever promise he made to his mother on her deathbed, about not harboring hatred, was of no use now. He knew Helene was incapable of harming her baby and that the rumors he heard circulating around town smelled of Josie's involvement. *This time you've gone too far.*

Up front, Amos continued to say a few words about the baby's short life.

Doc Nichols fumbled with the smelling salts capsule in his pocket.

Hanah felt wobbly and grabbed hold of Sam for support.

Annalee broke down in tears, joining the other sobbing women.

A few of the children rustled about impatiently. Aside from an occasional cough and crying, the place was still. The neighbor's dog stood quietly across the street watching. Trees were motionless and the sky was bare of birds when Amos finished his short talk and turned to Frank. "Do you want to say anything?"

Frank shook his head and remained silent.

Amos then looked over the group, down at the tiny closed coffin, up to the sky and said with tears streaming down his face, "He's in heaven now. He's at peace. Let us all pray that we find our own peace in these difficult times. Let's have a moment of silent prayer for Frank, Helene, and Mabel."

Heads bowed. Amos stood pensively for several minutes, then said, "Amen."

"Amen," the congregation followed.

Frank remained behind with the coffin as people filed out.

"What a shame," whispered Sam to his wife Hanah.

"I don't know how I'd live if it were our child," she replied.

"So young."

Satchel led Josie and their family away rapidly before she could make any comments to anyone.

Gus went back to his store and kept it closed. He went upstairs to his loft and poured himself a large glass of whiskey and thought of Frank back there at the coffin with his dead baby. For the first time in years, he broke down in tears.

*

A week had passed since the burial of little Frankie. Amos sat at his dining room table with Rebecca while their children played outside.

"Did they take Helene to Carson City yet?" she asked.

"Last night."

"Poor Frank. I can't even imagine what he's going through. Burying his little boy and now having to sign all those papers to admit her. Why'd he have to do that?"

"If he didn't sign, it could have gone to court. Not what any of them need right now."

"Court?"

"As long as there was suspicion of violence against her baby..."

Rebecca protested, "Helene loved her children. She'd never hurt..."

"Someone started that rumor. But to be honest, we don't know what goes on in people's homes. You think you know someone then something happens to tell you different."

"You can't honestly think she did this on purpose."

"I don't. I'm just saying that we don't really know what people are capable of. I counsel people. Oh God, you have no idea. We all think we're so smart, better than that guy over there who's doing no good, then something snaps. We don't know what's inside ourselves, let alone anyone else. We're all struggling with our emotions, wanting things to be different than they are. So much unrest in our souls, and yet we walk around lying about it all, putting on faces for our friends."

She reached a hand out to her husband. "You never told me anything."

"I can't, Becky. It wouldn't be right. The gossip stops here. All it does is create more damage."

"Poor Frank. What now?"

"The idea is for him to get a place in Carson City to be close to Helene."

"How in the world are they going to afford that?"

"Mildred."

"Mildred's doing that for them?"

"She's a good woman, Becky."

"What about Mabel?"

"She's staying at Charley's till they know about Helene."

"Know what?"

"Whether she's going to come out of the state she's in."

"Oh dear Lord."

*

The weeks that followed brought with them the space needed for a return to normal, just as Charley had hoped for that night at Mildred's. With the help of the women, he moved Mabel and Cranky in with him. He did his best to take care of his niece, to occupy her with playful activities and spoil her with trips to Gus's. He was grateful it took very little time for her to get back into the typical life of a child.

"Let's go play on the swing."

Charley smiled. "You're gonna wear me out."

"Let's go! Come on, Uncle Charley!"

"I guess we have some time before we head out to Mildred's. On your mark. Get set. Go!" He ran for the door with Mabel and Cranky behind him and headed for the swings in the schoolyard.

Charley pushed and watched her fly through the air. *We sure did save each other, didn't we? Would any of this have happened if Mildred hadn't brought you around to me? You're safe with me, Mabel. For as long as I live. Did you hear that, Emma?*

They finished playing then went back to Charley's to get ready for a visit to Mildred's.

Mabel said, "I have to get Cranky's things ready."

Charley smiled. "Now what would those be?"

Mabel ran to where she slept and pulled a sack out from under her bed. She ran back to Charley. "Here!"

"What do you have there?"

Mabel became excited. "Look."

Charley looked and broke out in laughter. He brought out a ball and held up a knotted rag. "Where'd you get this?"

"Mildred! We made it together." She excitedly explained they used rope, material, and string to make a toy for the dog.

"What's it for?"

"Pulling! It's Cranky's favorite toy."

"And this?" He held a piece of bark.

"Auntie Dra gave that to Cranky."

"Oh, Auntie Edra did, did she?"

"Yeah. For catch." She gathered Cranky's toys, put them back in the sack, and insisted, "Let's go!"

They stopped by Gus's to pick up some biscuits before continuing on to Mildred's.

"Well, well, if it isn't my favorite little customer."

"I'm not little. Tell him, Uncle Charley. Look how tall I am." Mabel walked over to the nearest wall and put her back to it. Charley knew the drill on measuring her height.

"Why Mabel, you've grown a whole inch since you were last here," joked Gus.

"I'll take that tin over there." Charley pointed to the biscuits he wanted.

Mabel ran around to the candy aisle and grabbed hold of several hard candies. "I want these." She handed them to Gus.

Gus put the candy in a little bag. "Here you are. On the house."

Mabel reached in, grabbed a candy and put one in her mouth.

Gus said with affection, "Hey, young lady, you'll ruin your dinner." Turning to Charley, he said, "You heading out to Mildred's now?"

"Yes, we are," replied Charley as Mabel grabbed him by the arm. "Let's go. Cranky's waiting."

"One minute," Charley said, and then leaned over and spoke to Gus briefly under his breath.

On the ride out Charley asked, "How's about singing me a song?"

Mabel giggled and broke out in "Mary Had a Little Lamb."

Charley sang along, "Whose fleece was white as…"

Cranky started barking at the familiar sight of the Dunlap's roadway. Mildred and Edra were outside in the yard waiting for them. Cranky jumped from the buggy before it stopped and ran up to greet them. Mabel squealed, "Mildred! Dra! We're here!"

Edra laughed at the way Mabel pronounced her name. "Who in a million years could have planned this?" she said to Mildred. "Come on over here and give Auntie Dra her hug."

Mabel gave them both hugs and ran into the house. Charley gave Mildred and Edra his own hug. "She's perky today," he laughed.

Mabel yelled from the house, "Chocolate cake!"

Mildred laughed. "Oh no! We better get in there before all the cake's gone."

They went inside to find Mabel with chocolate cake smeared over her mouth. Cranky sat beside her with a look that said, *Where's mine?*

Charley said to Mildred, "I took the liberty and invited another friend over."

Mildred laughed. "Now who would that be?"

"Gus."

194

"Illusion is the first of all pleasures." OSCAR WILDE

27

Fall moved into a cold winter. When the snow melted, spring produced lupines dancing in the sunlight. The temperate season brought with it a beauty and with the warmth came the return of the loons to Walker Lake. Like the desert tortoise, which heads underground into tunnels with the start of cold and returns when the frost melts, rattlers came out from hibernating under rocks and burrows and begin to mate and find their prey.

Annalee, Hanah, Sarah and Josie sat at Barney's Cafe sipping cups of tea.

Annalee asked, "Did you see that new customer over at Gus's?"

"The one that moved into the Whitmore's place?" asked Sarah.

"I just saw them," said Josie.

"And?" asked Hanah.

"Finegold. Irving and Edith. Satchel sent a telegram for them yesterday after they arrived to let their family know they are here."

"What'd it say?" Annalee asked.

"I just told you," Josie said, adding sarcastically, "sounds like a Jewish name to me. Why in the world would a Jew want to move into our Protestant town? Isn't there enough land in this world for them to go where they're wanted?"

Annalee said, "Well at least they're not living in town."

"Good company for Mildred," Josie laughed. "All those church haters."

Hanah picked up the gingerbread cookie sitting on her plate and took a bite. "I have to get Pat's recipe. These are so good. Must be the extra vanilla extract." She wiped her mouth and the remaining crumbs from her hands with a napkin and took a sip of tea. "What's happening with Charley?"

"He's heading to Carson City in a couple of days with Mabel," replied Sarah.

Hanah commented, "That poor little girl. Having a mother in the mad house. Good thing they got Charley around to take care of her."

Josie struck out, "Helene brought it on herself. Why, I never liked her."

"You never told us that," Hanah retorted.

"She started that false rumor about Charley and Mildred. This whole mess...it's on her head."

Annalee became indignant. "I remember it was you who started that, Josie."

"Me? Why would I do that? She's his sister-in-law. She's the one in the crazy house."

"Mildred's done for," commented Sarah. "She's never going to find another man like Charley."

"Too bad we didn't see her when she was pregnant," smirked Josie.

"She wasn't pregnant..." Hanah began.

Josie countered, interrupting, "Yes she was. I heard it from Doc. She miscarried."

"Doc wouldn't say that," Hanah objected indignantly.

"Yes he would and he did. Not directly...but I have it from a reliable person," Josie fumed, covering up the lie.

Hanah propitiated by saying nothing further.

"Maybe Mildred will go be with Charley," Sarah said.

"She'll never leave this town. Her daddy's money helped build this place," insisted Annalee.

Hanah added, "I heard she helped Sherriff Roper out last winter..."

"Her daddy. Her daddy. He robbed the landowners blind. He swindled rightful owners out of their property. Mildred hoarding all that money. Why she's a no good selfish pig. Making all the rest of us struggle to put bread on our tables. She'll never leave her place and her miserable cousin!" Josie's face turned ruddier than ketchup. "With all that money, she has to go and rent to Jews!"

Annalee appeared preoccupied when she asked, "Do you think Helene did it on purpose?"

Sarah responded, "Why wouldn't she? She wanted Mildred's money. She thought if she married Charley off to her, she'd…"

Annalee interrupted, "I didn't mean that."

"Well what'd you mean then?" asked Sarah.

"I meant the baby."

*

A couple of days later, the telegraph office was visited by two businessmen who had ridden in from Carson City. Tobias and Bradford had their orders. They also had the power. They were known throughout Carson City and its outlying towns as two brokers you do not mess around with. Satchel was instantly intimidated when they handed him their business cards.

"I think you better lock your door, Mr. Purdue." Tobias moved his face close to Satchel's.

Satchel took a hard noisy swallow that told the men how nervous he felt. He complied and then waited with trepidation.

"This offer is to be kept between us," said Bradford.

Satchel wiped beads of sweat from his forehead. "What offer you talking about?"

"A clerk's position in Carson City at the telegraph office is what you tell people. Mr. Tobias here has the contract."

Tobias took a sheet of paper out of his pocket, unfolded it, and placed it on the desk before Satchel.

Satchel's eyes met a blank piece of paper. "I don't understand?" He soaked in a slow deliberate breath, looking back and forth at the two men. "This some kind of joke?"

197

"No joke, Mr. Purdue," said Tobias.

Satchel stuttered, "There's...there's...nothing here."

"Exactly. Nothing more powerful than an empty slate. Don't you ever forget that. One word from you about this and that's what your life will become. Nothing. And that includes your wife."

"But..." Satchel's gut knotted tighter. "People will have seen you both come in here. What do I tell them?"

"As I said, a clerk's position in Carson City at the telegraph office and if word gets out otherwise, we will see to it that you won't get a job in any reputable city in this State."

Satchel stood speechlessly, fear washing over him.

"Mr. Purdue, we expect you to be packed and in Carson City by tomorrow evening," stated Bradford firmly.

Satchel stood there shaking his head in disbelief. "But...but..."

The two men had walked to the door to let themselves out when Tobias turned back with a serious look and said, "One more thing, Mr. Purdue. You better learn to keep that wife of your's mouth shut."

Satchel whispered, "Josie!"

Gus stood on the porch of his store and smiled to himself as he watched Tobias and Bradford mount their horses and ride out of town.

When word got out later that Satchel had been offered a telegraph office position in Carson City, the townspeople were surprised that he had accepted the offer so quickly. One individual was not, and that was Gus who had recently been made a silent business partner in the properties owned by Mildred.

✳

The day before they were to leave for Carson City, Charley brought Mabel and Cranky by for a visit with Mildred and Edra. They were waiting on the front porch when Charley and Mabel arrived.

"There they are," smiled Edra as she held up a gaily-wrapped package.

Mabel jumped from the buggy and ran to them. "That for me?" She grabbed for the package.

"It's a very special gift, my sweetheart," smiled Edra. Over the last

198

several months, she had grown very fond of Mabel.

"Oh boy! I can't wait!" Mabel cried happily as she ripped at the wrapping.

Charley had come with his own wrapped gift. "Well, lookie here. We've got an early Christmas."

"Charley, you've done enough for us."

Edra knelt down to give Mabel a hug and watch her open her gift. "This is something you can wear all your life and never forget your Auntie Mildred and Auntie Dra."

Mabel tore off the rest of the paper to find a small box, which she quickly opened. She pulled out a sterling chain necklace with a heart-shaped locket. "Mine! Oh Auntie Dra! This is so pretty! Thanks!"

"Aren't you going to thank your Auntie Mildred?" asked Charley.

Mabel hugged Mildred who said, "You can open it."

Mabel fumbled with the tiny latch and popped open the locket. "Look, Uncle Charley."

Charley saw inside the locket were two miniature photo portraits, Edra on one side and Mildred on the other. "That's a beauty. So nice of you. Here, I brought you something also." He handed his package to Mildred. "There's a little something in there for each of you."

Mildred unwrapped the box and opened it. Inside were two small blue mugs with white embossing. "Why Charley, these are Wedgwood." Mildred knew these were treasures that must be a hundred years old. "My mamma left me some Wedgwood plates. Look just like these mugs."

Her mother had told her the story of Josiah Wedgwood who had worked with an established potter until the mid-eighteenth century. It was his marriage to a remote cousin and her sizeable dowry that had enabled him to start his own pottery business. Mildred had often looked at their plates and thought about her own inheritance. She knew that it would never become a dowry. She sometimes reflected on the irony that Wedgwood had married his cousin.

"I thought I saw those plates here." Charley reflected on something Gus had loaned him to read about the history of Wedgwood. He smiled

THE PERSECUTION OF MILDRED DUNLAP

at Mildred and wondered if they were thinking the same thing.

"Charley, this is the perfect gift for us. Look, Edra."

When it was time to say their final good-byes and give their last hugs, all except Mabel fought back tears. Mildred could barely get out the words, "Come back soon, you hear?"

Mildred and Edra watched the dust spill over the wheels of Charley's buggy as they drove away. Just as they were almost out of earshot, they heard Cranky's bark.

Mildred thought, *Thank you, my friend, for everything you helped us with, especially encouraging Edra to go town. Couldn't have done it without you. All that worry is gone and thankfully I have my life and health back. Never knew holding so much inside could break the body down. Never again.*

As the women turned to go back inside, Mildred gave Edra's buttocks a pat.

Edra picked up her pace and lilted, "Don't be getting too frisky with me in public," she laughed.

Mildred smiled, "Gus won't mind."

✳

Mildred and Edra sat at Gus's dining table and watched as he placed tea and chocolate cake in front of them.

"Ladies, please help yourselves."

Mildred poured the tea.

"You're looking well, Mildred?"

"Thankfully Gus, I am."

"I'm glad to hear it. You've been through a lot."

Edra commented, "I finished *Moby Dick* last night."

"Did you read it, Mildred?"

"Yes, I read it first. Thanks so much for the loan."

They talked into the evening about the book, an adventurous whaling voyage that had become a vehicle for examining such themes as obsession, the nature of evil, and the human struggle against the elements.

"Oh look! How beautiful and peaceful!" exclaimed Mildred.

All attention shifted to the window and the foothills beyond that were slowly and gently turning a magnificent red hue as the warm comforting sun set on Red River Pass.

Epilogue

On May 19, 1897, Oscar Wilde was released from prison. He spent the last three years of his life in France in a self-imposed exile from society and artistic circles under a pseudonym. Although he was penniless, he was able to pursue the uninhibited pleasures that he had been denied in England.

He died of meningitis on November 30, 1900, with his friend Reggie Turner at his bedside.

"Love is fed by the imagination, by which we become wiser than we know, better than we feel, nobler than we are: by which we can see Life as a whole: by which, and by which alone, we can understand others in their real as in their ideal relations."

OSCAR WILDE

44470611R00114

Made in the USA
Middletown, DE
09 June 2017